90
MILES TO
FREEDOM

K.C. HILTON

90
MILES TO
FREEDOM

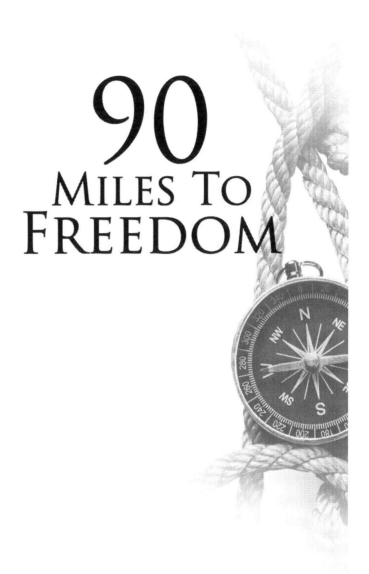

K.C. HILTON

Dedication

This book is dedicated to the thousands of people that had a dream of a better life. They journeyed across rough waters and endured harsh elements, with dreams filled with hope. Some found their freedom in America. And others made the ultimate sacrifice trying. Hundreds were turned away and returned to their country, only to suffer the consequences. Your strength and courage will never be forgotten.

Acknowledgements

My critique group:

Ashlee for your tears and encouragement.

Brian for your honesty.

Eric for your excitement and enthusiasm.

Chris, my awesome husband and best friend, for keeping the humour flowing and insisting that George stole your identity.

Collin had the perfect life. He had a loving family and everything money could buy. A life envied by all.

But Collin wasn't perfect. He had a secret, one that came with a price. A secret that could destroy his life and everyone in it.

Chapter 1

May 2010

"George!" Betty yelled up the stairs. "We have to go! We're going to be late! And we still have to buy Joey a graduation card! What on earth are you doing up there?"

George and Betty Scott weren't old enough to retire, but they didn't need to work, either. They'd wisely invested in commodities and made a mint when oil prices went through the roof.

They'd always loved the ocean. When they found themselves financially secure with no mortgage, no car payments and nothing else to worry about save living expenses, they decided to sell their old home and move so they could raise their two boys near the water. When their oldest son was still in high school they purchased a home just outside of Key West, Florida in a subdivision called Key Haven.

George and Betty loved Key Haven. They were perfectly happy to live in Key Haven for the rest of their lives. All they wanted was to make their children happy, grow old together, and patiently wait to spoil future grandchildren.

Their two story home sat on a large lot, the back of it facing the Gulf. The house was huge. At thirty-five hundred square feet, it was comprised of three bedrooms, three and a half baths, and a two car garage.

Most women are generally interested in having a large kitchen, and Betty's was larger than most. However, her favorite feature of the house was that she could walk through the French doors in the living room and step onto the stone-tiled patio. The patio led to the seawall, which was exactly forty feet away from their private boat docks.

Betty loved to sit on her patio for hours at a time, watching the water. The Gulf was so clear that she could see the fish swimming deep within, flitting here and there in their underwater world. Schools of dolphins swimming by in the early mornings or late afternoons were an added bonus that made Betty smile every time.

The backyard patio area was George and Betty's second home. They found no need to go anywhere for vacations.

"No need to take a vacation now that we live here. Most people spend loads of money just so they can vacation where we live," George and Betty often said to their children. "Besides, where on earth could there possibly be a more beautiful place to visit?"

George was more than intrigued by his two car garage. The large area kept him contentedly busy, organizing and storing his handyman tools and miscellaneous items. George, being an efficient man, had labeled all the drawers and cabinets in the garage so he could quickly and easily locate whichever particular tool he might need. He had a full arsenal of the tools a man would need to do odd jobs around the home, and was very proud of them. The labels were also helpful for Betty, because she was often more inclined to use the handle of a screwdriver to hang pictures throughout their home rather than take the time to search for a hammer. She often told George that "if it works, that's all that matters."

Most of George and Betty's time was spent on their partially covered back patio, reading books, playing games on their laptops, and discussing the day's events. Often they lazed in their in-ground swimming pool or in the attached Jacuzzi, following up with a delicious meal which George cooked on their gas grill. Evening sunsets offered the most glorious setting, more fascinating than any movie. The ocean not only offered endless hours of mesmerizing views, but also provided tranquil sounds that soothed their already contented souls.

George was a tall man, just over six feet tall, and had a slender but muscular build. He wore his straight brown hair in a shaggy style and sported what he considered to be a very stylish goatee. He always made mention to anyone who would listen that if he didn't have facial hair he would look twenty years younger.

The top of Betty's head almost reached George's shoulder, since she stood only a couple of inches over five feet. When George told people about his facial hair making him look older, she was always pleased to chip in that if she were only seventy five pounds lighter she would also look twenty years younger. And Betty never minded when George teased her about being short. She simply responded by telling him she wasn't short at all. Technically, she was vertically challenged. She also told him she wasn't overweight; she had thick skin.

The couple was immensely proud of their two sons, Collin and Joey.

Collin, their oldest, was twenty-four. He was half a foot shorter than his father, with a stocky build that showed a bit of muscle. His hair was brown, like that of both his parents. He wore it in a fade style cut, keeping a little extra hair on top and using hair gel for the wet, messy look. Collin also wore a well-groomed goatee. On his left ear he sported a small gold ball earring.

When he'd graduated from high school, Collin told his parents he had decided not to attend college. Instead, he wanted to own his own business. Rather than his parents paying for his college tuition, he asked if they could save money and purchase him a seaworthy fishing boat. He astutely pointed out that owning a ship like that would ensure he always had work, a place to sleep and, of course, an abundance of seafood, so he would never go hungry. Collin had worked on various fishing boats throughout high school, learning as much as he could. Betty and George were well aware that he had always dreamed of owning one of his own.

So now Collin was the owner of a large fishing boat, in which he lived and worked, making a great living by charging vacationing tourists for fishing excursions.

Chapter 2

On the morning of Joey's graduation, Collin felt somewhat sluggish. He had not slept all night, explaining to his parents that the fishing tourists had paid him double the night before so that he would take them fishing during the night hours. The tourists claimed that fishing at night during a full moon would allow them to catch the best of fish.

Collin had planned on taking a short nap before graduation to ensure he'd be able to keep his eyes open during Joey's ceremony, as well as at the planned celebration dinner afterwards. He knew his parents had made reservations at their favorite restaurant. Collin also wanted to be wide enough awake to meet up with his fiancée, Morgan, after dinner.

But for now the focus was on Joey's high school graduation. Betty paced around the front entrance of their house, impatient to get moving. Collin stood on the side, watching her and smiling.

"Lord help me! That wretched man! He will be the death of me yet! How ironic that the general consensus is that women take too much time getting ready. Well apparently," Betty shouted through the door, aiming her voice in the direction of their bedroom, "the general consensus hasn't met my husband!"

"Mom, it'll be fine," Collin assured her. "You know how Dad gets on special occasions."

She ignored her son, choosing instead to encourage her husband with a little more yelling. "George! Why is it that I'm always waiting for you to get ready? Isn't it supposed to be the other way around?"

"I'm coming, I'm coming," puffed George, sounding out of breath. He hurried through the hall holding two pairs of shoes. His tie hung undone around his neck. "What do you think: black or brown?"

"Either pair will do just fine," Betty snapped. She bit her lower lip, trying to hold back her anger. "It's not like anyone will notice the color of your shoes anyway!"

George gave his son a bewildered look, then shrugged and rushed back to their bedroom. They could hear him dropping the shoes onto the floor.

"You're worse than a girl going on her first date!" Betty shouted, then looked over at Collin. She shook her head and chuckled under her breath. "God help us."

Collin laughed, always entertained by his parents' strange little ways. Their good-hearted sarcasm could be very funny, and they seemed to get great joy out of picking at each other most every day.

It wouldn't be the least bit out of the ordinary to hear either of them say, "I'm going to kick your ass," then start laughing and peck the other one on the lips.

George came shuffling out of their bedroom in his black shoes, mumbling while he tried to fix his tie. "I just want everything to be perfect. Our little boy is graduating from high school and will be off to college after the summer." The tie appeared to be fighting back, so Betty stepped over to give him a hand. "Our little boy, Betty! He's turning into a man so fast. He's just barely out of diapers! Well ..." he said, pausing and tilting his head to the side. "Maybe not diapers. Maybe that's pushing it. But how can it be that we're already headed to his high school graduation? When did he grow up so fast?"

Betty smiled and kept quiet, letting George go on and on, thinking out loud.

Suddenly George's eyes lit up like a kid's on Christmas morning. He grinned from ear to ear. "Maybe Joey can buy a boat after Collin sells the yacht. Then he could use the other side of the dock. Now that's a great idea!"

Joey was eighteen and stood six feet tall, like his father. He had a slender build and enjoyed teasing his older brother about being short. Of course teasing in this family was always done with affection, so Collin was never upset when Joey went after him.

Height wasn't the only difference between the brothers. Joey was graduating from high school at the top of his class and had completely different plans from what Collin had after graduating.

Joey wanted nothing more than to attend Florida Tech to obtain a degree in Oceanography. He loved the ocean, its creatures and everything else about it. He found it all extremely intriguing. Joey could often be found reading and studying every article he could find about what went on under the sea.

"Having an ocean as a backyard is better than a fenced in yard with grass and a swimming pool," Joey would say when people asked him where he might live in the future. "Besides, I wouldn't care much for mowing a large yard of grass."

When George's tie was finally knotted properly, Betty got behind him and shooed him toward the door, clicking her tongue as she went.

"I'm not sure why you're having Empty Nest Syndrome symptoms, George. After all, you are hoping our boys will continue to live at home, right?" She grabbed the keys to the car and rushed towards the door. "It's not as if living on a boat which is docked in our backyard is exactly moving out, you know!"

George ignored her comment, continuing instead to mumble and complain about how quickly his boys had grown into men. Collin stood in the living room, watching all the commotion. He was planning to go on his own to the graduation a little later on.

"Let's go, old man," Betty said when George hesitated in the doorway. "We're not getting any younger. Joey will never forgive us if we're late!"

"But -" George started.

Betty let out a sigh and rolled her eyes. "Oh, for Pete's sake. God help us. Get in the car!"

"When this is over, remind me why I married you. I'll need to remember so I don't kick your ass before the end of this day!" George said, chuckling. He gave Betty a light slap on her backside while they were walking through the door, and she answered with a flirtatious wink. He pulled the door closed behind him, then gave it a wiggle to make sure it was locked. Collin could hear his father talking through the door.

"Don't worry, old woman. We have three hours before graduation starts. I'm fairly sure we'll not only get a front row seat, but a front row parking spot as well!"

Chapter 3

George and Betty hurried down the front walkway and Collin, who was watching his parents through the large bay window, smiled when he witnessed his father open Betty's door for her. Such a sweet gesture, he thought, reminding himself to do that with Morgan later on. Once Betty was in the car, George walked around to the driver's side and closed his own door. Then they just sat there in the driveway, not going anywhere.

Collin yawned and peered out, wondering why they hadn't moved. He could see them in the car, looking at each other and talking, but the car hadn't even started up. It was strange that his mother was allowing them to simply sit there after she'd been in such a hurry before.

All of a sudden George and Betty bolted out of the vehicle and raced back to the house. Collin nearly laughed out loud at how entertaining all this was, but restrained himself to a low chuckle. The front door smashed open and slammed into the wall, making so much noise Collin thought it could have been mistaken for the police knocking down the front door during a raid.

"Collin! Collin!" Betty yelled shrilly.

21

She was panting as if she had just finished her first marathon. Collin frowned, feeling a flicker of concern over his mother. It was completely out of the ordinary for Betty to lose her composure, and her anxiety at that moment had certainly risen to a new level. George kept a close, fast pace behind his wife, almost bumping into her when she stopped short.

"Our car won't start!" she said. "Can we borrow your car?"

George appeared to be a little nervous, too, which was unusual. Collin could see him fidgeting in his pockets; he appeared noticeably uneasy.

"Yes, of course," Collin quickly replied, handing his father the keys. "But how will I get to Joey's graduation?"

Betty spun around to face George, and anyone could have heard a pin drop in the midst of the silence that suddenly filled the front hall. If looks could actually kill, Collin mused to himself. The entire scene was so unexpected and comedic that Collin wanted to laugh. He didn't, though. It didn't look like anyone else would think it was funny.

"Call Triple A," George muttered. "The number is in the phone book. I was planning to get a new battery this week, but I never got around to actually doing it."

George kept his eyes on Collin, out of the range of Betty's

22

piercing glare. Even so, Collin could swear he saw a hint of a nervous grin showing at the corner of his dad's mouth.

He will never hear the end of this, Collin thought to himself. He still fought the urge to laugh, but knew that if he gave in to the mirth he would have to endure his mom's wrath for many days to come.

George's expression changed very subtly when he caught a glimpse of Collin laughing under his breath. At first he started to flush with embarrassment, but before long he apparently saw the humor in the situation. George started to giggle, then quickly covered the sound with a loud cough. He thumped his chest with his fist for added effect.

It was easy for Collin to envision his dad listening to his mom's uninterrupted complaints all the way to graduation. He was so relieved that it was his father on the end of his mother's fury, not him or Joey. It made Collin even happier that he wasn't going to the graduation with them.

Oh, how fun this week was going to be, Collin thought, feeling only slightly sorry for his dad. His dad didn't make too many mistakes, usually, so he fully intended to play this one to the hilt. Teasing his father about this was going to provide great entertainment for awhile. He thought it might be that much more hysterical if he actually went to the auto parts store and picked up a battery himself, instead of calling Triple A. Yes, he decided. That's what he would do. He had time. By doing that, he would gain brownie points with his mom. Then he'd be able to sit back and watch his dad's expression while his mom raved about how wonderful Collin had gone out specifically to buy the battery.

It's not like George had a job or was working forty plus hours a week. He'd had more than enough time to have their car battery replaced. He was just too busy with his endless list of projects. Betty, on the other hand, kept busy with her lists, enjoying the whole process of planning events. Although it was only the middle of May, Betty's mind was already thinking of Christmas. She was constantly making notes of things that needed to be done, and what needed to be purchased. She searched the internet looking for good deals, always telling the others, "To get a good bargain, you should buy certain items during a certain time of the year." To prove her point, every year Betty bought Christmas wrapping paper after Christmas, usually at fifty to seventy-five per cent off.

"Don't worry about a thing, Mom," Collin told her, giving her a friendly wink. "I'll look after this and see you both at the graduation."

"Thanks, son. You're a star!" Betty said, smiling. She kissed Collin on the cheek and patted his arm as if he were a young boy. "Now don't forget to take your nap. And make sure you remember to set your alarm so you're not late." She kissed him again then ushered George once more toward the front door.

"We love you! See you there!" Betty called back over her shoulder.

Collin just smiled, then yawned again, stretching his arms up high so that he nearly touched the ceiling. A nap. That sounded perfect. He could definitely use some shut eye after the late night. He strolled towards the back door, headed for the dock. He had time to lie down before he was due at the ceremony.

At the exact moment in which Collin grabbed the handle and began to open the back door, the world exploded. The house rocked and the front windows smashed in, fragments shooting like knife-edged bullets down the hall and through the kitchen. Metal clanged against the roof and the walls and car alarms went off. Picture frames blew off the wall, and one of Betty's favorite lamps fell and shattered.

The impact of the blow threw Collin onto the floor, and he covered his head, seized by terror. Metal clanged, hammering the roof and the outside of the house. Car alarms sounded outside and the screams of terrified neighbors filled the street.

Chapter 4

Joey didn't find out until after graduation. He had waited among his friends and other graduating seniors, standing with their parents for at least a full hour after graduation. Several times he had tried to call his parents and Collin, and he had even sent text messages. None of them were answered.

In the end, Joey gave up searching through the huge crowd. The light mist that had hung over them all day was giving him a chill and making him even more miserable. They hadn't come. He'd hunted, but never found them, and didn't expect to find them now. Knowing his mother, if his parents had been there, they would have been in the front row, cheering him on. Now that evening was closing in, Joey decided to drive home.

This was really strange, their not being there. They had been talking about it for over a month now. His mom had even bought a new dress for the occasion. Very strange. Something important must have come up.

His mom would be upset because she hadn't been able to take any photos. She loved her scrapbooks. At least some of his friends had taken a few group shots, and he knew he'd appeared in some of those. He would ask his friends to email him some copies for his parents. It would be better than not having any at all, he thought.

Joey turned onto his street, but was forced to pull over. A policeman in a yellow raincoat was directing traffic, informing drivers that the road was closed.

Joey muttered something about it being his street and parked by the sidewalk. He got out of his car without bothering to either turn off the engine or close the door behind him. All his focus was on the horrifying scene before him. Red lights lit the early evening, bouncing from a slew of police cars and fire engines, hitting neighborhood houses, reflecting off windows and sparkling on the rain-dampened road. Yellow tape ordering bystanders "Do Not Cross" was strung along and across the road. Water hoses sprawled in a tangled mess.

Two ambulances were parked outside his home, their doors wide open. Except they weren't ambulances. Their side panels read: "Monroe County Coroner".

Joey headed towards the main hub of activity, moving more urgently as he realized everything seemed to convene in front of his house. The air around Joey's head felt funny, as if it buzzed - though that might just have been in his mind. He shook uncontrollably, feeling sick to his stomach.

Something bad had happened here. Something awful. Something life changing.

A local news van was parked in the middle of the street, within reach of a reporter who was talking to a camera. A crowd of neighbors gathered close in the surrounding yards, talking amongst each other, some crying openly.

In the blur of faces, Joey didn't recognize anyone. He looked around, searching for any kind of answer and his gaze fell upon the burned car in his family's driveway, still smoking.

"Oh my God," he whispered.

Then he saw Collin. He was on his knees, rolled into a ball in the neighbor's yard. Both of his hands covered his face and he sobbed helplessly through them, loud enough that everyone could hear. "Oh God!" he wept, saying it over and over.

Joey raced to his brother and skidded on his knees in the wet grass, stopping in front of Collin. "What's going on, Collin? What happened?" He grabbed Collin's shoulders and shook him, but Collin stayed hunched over, crying, unable to answer any of Joey's questions.

Joey shook him harder, unable to stop the tears that came to his eyes as well. "Collin! What happened? Collin! For God's sake, say something! Where are Mom and Dad?" Joey screamed.

Collin just rocked, sobbing.

Joey looked around, hoping for help. He shifted his eyes away from Collin and took in all of the emergency vehicles, the burned car smoking in front of their house. He continued to scan the area, desperately looking for his parents.

Then he saw them. His parents.

Two unidentifiable shapes, wrapped in black-zipped body bags. Someone in uniform was wheeling them to the coroner's vehicle. "Mom?" Joey managed to choke, scrambling to his feet. "Dad?"

He stumbled toward the coroner's vehicle, but could go no closer than a few steps before he leaned to the side and was violently ill. He straightened and spat to the side, watching through tear-filmed eyes as the coroner's vehicle shut its doors.

Having no idea what else to do, Joey turned and went back to Collin. He knelt beside his older brother, watching silently as the neighbors gawked with morbid curiosity and concern.

In the distance, beyond all the people and vehicles, Joey could hear a song playing on his car radio. He remembered he'd forgotten to shut it off, forgotten to close the door. The band on the radio were singing something familiar, a song with lyrics about "life being hard" or something like that. It seemed strangely fitting, that at that moment he could hear that song, those words. He would never forget that song. From that moment on, it would be infused deep into his memory.

Joey looked up as the light drizzle became more of a steady rain. Collin placed a hand on Joey's shoulder, and that was all it took for Joey to lose his self-control. He bawled like a baby, Collin's trembling arms wrapped around him.

"Everything will be okay, Joey," Collin whispered near Joey's ear. "I'll take care of you. Don't you worry. Everything will be okay. Do you hear me?"

Nothing would ever be the same.

Chapter 5

February 2010

A few months prior to Joey's graduation, George had secretly been eager to give Collin the money to purchase a used yacht he had found that needed work. George claimed it would be a partial advance of his inheritance and that it would also be a great turnaround investment for Collin. But for George, although he openly admitted to not having sea legs, there was an added bonus to giving Collin money for the yacht. Most homes in Key Haven made use of their boat slips or boat docks, located on the seawall, since they owned water crafts of varying shapes and sizes. When Collin tied his yacht to George's dock, it immediately gave the family social status among their neighbors.

Up until the point Collin had purchased the fishing boat and the yacht, George and Betty had only owned a few water crafts for the boys to use. Before that they couldn't bring themselves to purchase any type of boat because they were well aware that the boat would ultimately sit docked and doing nothing, thus being a waste of money.

Now Collin's fishing boat and yacht made use of both sides of the dock. Not only did the fishing boat provide a living place and a business, but the yacht brought Collin closer to his parents. They all enjoyed the actual process of working on the yacht, though Collin's younger brother, Joey, never took much interest in it. He was always busy with something else.

But Betty and George had a great time working on that yacht with Collin. Through it they found a new common interest they could all share. The work also gave George something different to add to his daily project list. As Collin had predicted, George looked forward to the new projects at hand and was thoroughly entertained by the whole thing. He was like a kid with a new toy.

When Collin had initially bought the yacht, it had been badly neglected. The boat needed a lot of simple, but time consuming, repairs, as well as an immediate deep cleaning. George had been secretly thrilled, though he frowned critically every time he discovered something that needed to be done. Collin knew his father always enjoyed a new project and was eager to get started.

Several cabinet door handles had been broken or gone missing. Fixtures needed to be replaced and they'd had to install new appliances in the galley. Flooring and carpet were all replaced, and everything that could be painted was given a fresh coat of paint. The outer seating needed to be reupholstered, and the hot tub was given some much needed repair on its motor as well as a replacement of the heating elements. Collin and his parents completed all of these things within the first few months of his buying the yacht.

When it came to cleaning and decorating, Betty had everything well under control. Like George, Betty was eager and excited to have something new to do outside of their typical daily routines. Within a few weeks, she had single-handedly cleaned and scrubbed the entire yacht, refusing to stop until she had achieved her high standards.

Collin and George cheered and applauded after Betty had finished vacuuming and wiping everything down on the yacht, but she would hear none of it. She dug in deep, scrubbing and cleaning every crevasse with determination. When she was finally finished with what she called the "sterilization" of the yacht, they were permitted to tell her how impressed they were. When they did, she simply waved her hand and smiled as if to say, "It was really nothing".

Despite her affinity for cleaning, there were some things with which she never got comfortable. One day, as she was dusting the lower shelves in the living quarters of the yacht, Collin and George heard Betty scream, and ran to her assistance.

"Spiders!" she squealed. "Oh, I hate spiders! How in the world did all these spiders get on a boat?"

They had rushed to see her at the first scream but relaxed when they witnessed her doing battle with the spiders. George had stood calmly at the side, arms crossed as he watched Betty swat at the spiders with her dusting towel. She made a funny little scream each time she struck at the shelves. George grinned, thoroughly enjoying the entertainment.

"Do spiders know how to swim or something? Ewww!" Betty howled again, swatting at another spider and missing it by a foot or more.

"Betty, my dear," George said, chuckling quietly. "Did I ever tell that you no matter where you sleep you will swallow an average of eight spiders per year?" He raised his eyebrows and Betty swept a cloud of dust from one of the upper shelves in his direction. He reached for a tissue to wipe his nose, then sneezed.

She glared at him, hands on her apron-clad hips. "Why would you ever go and tell me something like that? I didn't need to know that. Nobody wants to hear about spiders crawling in your mouth while you sleep. That's just plain gross. I can't believe you told me that!" She took a deep breath, then slowly let it out. "You know,

George, nobody, especially me, wants to hear any uninteresting or gross pieces of information. For future reference please keep that in mind."

She reluctantly got back to work dusting the shelves and remained on high alert for any spiders in the vicinity.

George nudged his son in the ribs. "I'll bet your mother wears a surgical mask to bed tonight," he said quietly.

Collin grinned. George loved to torment his wife, but only as long as it was funny. But two could play at that game. George sneezed again, and Betty turned around, a Cheshire cat grin on her face.

"Well, George, do you know that it's impossible to sneeze without closing your eyes?"

"No. No, I didn't know that one," George said, looking thoughtful. He paused and glanced up, as if he hoping for some kind of answer. "But do you know that falling coconuts kill an average of a hundred and fifty people every year?"

"Well, that's why we don't have any coconut trees in our yard," Betty bellowed. Her frown was gone and both she and George erupted into gales of laughter, hooting at each other until tears streamed down Betty's face. "And now you're going to hire an exterminator, George. I will never sleep again if I know we might have spiders. Those exterminators are going to check out the whole place, then they're going to keep on coming back every month."

It wasn't only cleaning that had Betty excited. She envisioned redecorating the entire yacht and thought that would be the most fun she had had in a long time. Betty loved to shop and could always find a great deal on almost anything. After they'd cleaned the yacht, she came home almost every day with bags upon bags of newly bought items. She was having the time of her life.

Betty was determined that the yacht should be well equipped with whatever a person might need, just in case someone felt a sudden urge to spontaneously take a little vacation. Betty had also mentioned that if a serious buyer came along, they would want a fully equipped yacht, ready to go at the drop of a dime. She called it the complete package, the "Yacht Al Fresco".

Chapter 6

Technically, Collin still lived at home with his parents; however, in his defense, he didn't actually live in his parents' home. Instead, he lived on his fishing boat, which just happened to be docked outside his parents' home almost every night.

Morgan, Collin's fiancée, was the love of his life. She occasionally dropped by when the family was working on the yacht on her days off. Morgan worked as a Registered Nurse at the Lower Keys Medical Center and had been working extra hours to help cover a fellow worker's vacation time. As a result, she and Collin hadn't been able to spend much time together over the past week.

Collin loved Morgan with all of his heart, and on the rare times he got to see her, he made big plans to show her just how much he'd missed her. It was pretty easy to make her happy, because they both loved the same thing. Whenever they made a date, he bought her some flowers, picked up Chinese take-out, and rented a few movies that they both had wanted to see. Then they'd relax on the couch at her apartment and he'd rub her tired feet. Of all those, Collin always knew Morgan would rank the latter at number one on her list.

Collin and Morgan had been engaged for over a year but hadn't yet set a date for the wedding. They had wanted to take their time and make sure they did everything right. Their first priority was to save enough money to purchase the right home. Morgan wanted to stay close to work, and Collin needed to have access to his fishing boat. His preference would be to have the boat docked just outside his back door, as was his parents' home, since fishing excursions were his means of income. Even though they hadn't quite saved up enough money, Collin and Morgan had attended a few open houses of homes for sale in Key Haven, wanting to get a better idea of the type of home they'd want and the cost. Both wanted to stay in Key Haven after they married, and Collin's parents couldn't be happier about that.

At first it had surprised Collin that the house was more of a priority to Morgan than having an extravagant wedding. In the end, the couple decided to hold a small, intimate wedding near the water. Their only guests would be immediate family members, and their reception would be a simple, fun barbecue at a nearby park.

Both of their mothers, were, of course, opposed to these simple reception plans. The two mothers spent many pleasant afternoons discussing their own version of the reception plans at Betty's favorite restaurant, the 'Roof Top Café'. In fact, they decided to go ahead and completely reorganize the reception, making sure they included little to no input from either Collin or Morgan. They wanted to do it on their own.

Betty loved to rave about their plans. "This will be the best reception anyone has ever seen. There is no way anyone will be able to call this a 'simple' reception."

Morgan was always happy to help Collin and his parents while they worked on the yacht. More often than not, Morgan found herself working side by side with Betty, and the two women enjoyed hours of laughter and chat, talking about Collin's childhood.

Betty didn't always have the family photo albums handy to pull out and share, but she did have interesting tales to tell. Morgan adored Collin, and was all ears every time Betty told a story. She was intrigued by every tiny detail of Collin's life. Betty had no problem opening up and telling everyone the most humorous and embarrassing stories. Once she started telling her stories there was no stopping her.

"Well," Betty began one time, "we always knew that Collin was going to be an entrepreneur. We've known that ever since he was in grade school. He went about it in the most ingenious ways. One of my favorite stories is about the time when he brought his entire allowance to a small general store. He purchased a ton -"

"Not a ton, Mom," Collin objected.

"Oh, all right. At least a few pounds of candy. You know the ones? The long clear plastic wrappers that held multiple colors of little chocolate covered round candies."

Morgan frowned. "But how did that make him -"

Betty held up her hand. "Just wait. It gets better. You'll understand in a minute. The next morning before the school bus arrived, Collin had stuffed his backpack full of the candy. I remember that. It was full to the brim along with all of his books. I figured he was taking it to school to share with all of his friends."

"Mom ... " Collin started. Betty smiled sweetly and waggled her finger at him like she always had. He just shook his head and grinned, knowing what was to come.

"That afternoon," Betty continued. "I got a call from the principal of the school." She chuckled, then set her face in an expression of astonishment and looked right at Morgan. "Can you imagine? Apparently Collin was selling the candy for ten cents apiece! The kids were using their lunch money to buy the candy from him!"

"That bastard principal!" Collin interrupted. Betty and Morgan glanced his way, startled. "He took the rest of my candy and all the freaking money!"

Everyone laughed and teased Collin, who was a very good sport about it all.

"Okay. Okay. That's enough of the stories for one day," Collin said, trying to take the attention off himself. He was fairly embarrassed and had a feeling Morgan was probably only laughing to be polite.

"Oh, Collin," Betty purred, smiling that smile that Collin could never refuse. "One more story can't hurt."

"Yes please! I want to hear more," Morgan exclaimed. Her eyes shone with laughter.

Collin couldn't possibly refuse, despite the fact that he was at the receiving end of all the teasing. The two women he loved most in the world were enjoying themselves to no end. No matter the story that was told, it was a wonderful feeling to see them both happy. Even his father, who was still painting the side of the boat, looked like he was having a good time.

"Okay," Collin announced, giving them all a big-hearted smile. "One more story." He looked over at his Dad, his eyes pleading for help, but none was offered. "I don't think I could handle much more embarrassment beyond that."

George chuckled, not looking up from the fresh white paint he'd just spread. "Sucker," he silently mouthed at Collin.

"You're getting a kick out of this aren't you, old man?" Collin growled.

George said nothing, but his eyes danced. He gazed at the ceiling, whistling a quirky little tune. He pretended he hadn't heard Collin just so he could pester his son even more.

Betty reached over to the radio and slid in a CD, then pressed play. Romantic music flowed through the speakers and filled the room with words about someone hoping not to fall in love.

"What is it," Collin asked with a smile, "about that song that makes you realize just how much you love the people that you love?"

"Have I ever told you the 'Bucket' story?" Betty asked Morgan, her voice smooth as liquid honey. Morgan shook her head and smiled with encouragement.

Chapter 7

God, she was beautiful. Every time Collin looked at Morgan he fell more in love with her. He was the luckiest man in the world. He watched her reactions while his mother told her another embarrassing story he'd heard a million times, and heard it brand new through Morgan's ears. His heart melted a little more every time he looked at her.

Collin loved hearing his mother and father laugh. And hearing Morgan laugh with them was the most wonderful sound he could imagine. He could tell Morgan enjoyed teasing him as well, and smiled. He would never hear the end of it. The relentless teasing would begin before they were even married.

Just the thought of Morgan becoming his wife made Collin a happier man. He could put up with endless teasing just for that honor.

"Oh, Collin!" Betty suddenly exclaimed, clapping her hands. "You're going to have such beautiful children!"

Morgan and Collin exchanged a startled glance, then Collin watched with fascination as Morgan turned a healthy shade of red. He wasn't entirely surprised by his mother's outburst. She was generally compelled to say things like that. It's just that usually she waited until after Morgan had left.

"Morgan is so gorgeous and oh, such a wonderful girl," she would say. "Charming, delightful, attractive ... I couldn't be any happier for you. You have made a wonderful choice, deciding to marry Morgan. You are both going to be so happy." Then she'd turn to George, her eyes gleaming with happiness. "Isn't that right, George?"

This was the first time she'd said anything like that with Morgan still around, but her outburst caused only the tiniest break in the conversation. Betty didn't seem to sense any awkwardness at all. Collin stole a glance at his father, who was still pretending not to hear. But Collin saw his secret smile. He continued to paint, waiting to hear the outcome of this conversation.

"Yes, Mother. I completely agree with you on all counts," Collin said, smiling at his mother. "But may I add a few of my own descriptions of Morgan?"

Betty narrowed her eyes, suspicious that Collin was up to something, then nodded when she realized there was no way on earth Collin would embarrass Morgan. She cocked her right eyebrow, warning her son to behave and be nice. "By all means Collin, I would love to hear your portrayal of your future wife."

Morgan blushed ferociously, sensing the attention coming her way. She was used to this demonstrative family, though, and completely at home in the midst of them.

"Well," Collin said, then cleared his throat. "We shall begin with the obvious. Morgan is a delicate five feet tall with long, gorgeous brown hair. She barely wears any makeup at all, because she doesn't need any. She is naturally perfect."

"So sweet of you," Morgan said. "You can stop now."

Collin gave Morgan a smile which clearly said "I love you" without the need for words. Then he shook his head. "I'm sorry, Morgan, but there's more."

She put her hands over her face, hiding, but giggling.

Collin continued, addressing his audience of three as formally as if he were speaking to a stadium full of people. "As you can see, Morgan is more than just stunning. She is breathtaking." Collin glanced towards his mother, whose eyes were sparkling, her mouth slightly open as she took in her son's words. He took his fiancée's hand in his and returned his full concentration to Morgan, kissing the top of her hand before continuing. "Morgan moves me like no other woman ever has. She has taken over my mind and my soul." Collin's chest tightened, seeing Morgan's beautiful eyes well up.

George stopped painting and glanced toward Betty and Collin. Betty dabbed at the corners of her eyes, sniffling at her son's beautiful tribute. George smiled, watching his romantic wife. Based on the speech Collin had just made, it was obvious that he had inherited some of those traits from his mother. George was what Collin called a "closet romantic". He'd never admit to enjoying those emotions, though he did feel them. George didn't usually declare such feelings in front of anyone, except for when he was all alone with Betty. Collin and Joey knew all about it from the times Betty occasionally enlightened them, giving them her own version of the story. He figured his dad would be glad to know that he'd given her something to brag about.

Betty had taught her sons well. She often preached to them about loving a woman for more than just her outward appearance. She often told the boys that "the gem within a woman is the most precious jewel you will ever discover."

All this romance had settled the mood into something resembling calm. Apparently George felt the need to put a stop to that. It was time to laugh again.

"Okay, Collin," he said, waving his paint brush vaguely in Betty's direction. "I've heard the romantic version of Morgan, which your mother would want to hear. Now give me the version a son would tell his father, a.k.a. me." George smiled from ear to ear, waiting for Collin's reply. Collin glanced nervously at Morgan, but she only giggled with encouragement.

"Well," Collin said, then shot a tentative grin at George. He wasn't quite sure what might be appropriate to say in front of his parents. Especially while Betty continued to murmur something along the lines of, "That's my boy. Romantic at heart. I taught him well. Yes, I did."

"I'm waiting," George teased.

Collin cleared his throat, then smiled. He knew perfectly well that all his father wanted was for him to make his mother gasp. "Well," he repeated, "I would probably tell a.k.a. you that my Morgan is not only adorable and gorgeous, but that she is also very passionate."

"Passionate and adorable," George repeated slowly, testing the feel of the words in his mouth. "Yeah. For sure. That's what I would want in the bedroom. I gotta tell you, son, 'passionate and adorable' sounds like something out of one of those romance novels your mother is always reading." He chuckled, then shook his head, looking sadly disappointed. "Tsk tsk, boy. You can do better than that."

"George!" Betty cried, using her firmest, most disapproving tone.

"Come on. Have I ever called you passionate and adorable?" George raised both eyebrows, waiting for Betty to reply, but she only narrowed her eyes at him and said nothing. Her expression very clearly said that she wanted to strangle George. Her husband smiled smugly. "No. I thought not. I use more vivacious words to describe you, my love."

Betty still said nothing, but continued to glare at him as if to warn him not to say another word. But George was having way too much fun. She knew she couldn't stop him even if she tried.

"Well? On out with it, Collin! Let's hear it. I haven't got all day … well, actually, maybe I do. But that's beside the point."

Collin began again, trying desperately not to blush. "Morgan is … she is … " He squinted, then glanced at Morgan, who was watching him with a wide-eyed grin.

"Well, all right, Dad," he said, keeping his mischievous eyes on his fiancée. "But keep calm. I wouldn't want you to have a coronary or anything." Collin paused, stumbling to find the right words. In the end he decided to color it a bit, to lighten the mood, and did so by speaking with a strong British accent. "My Morgan is sexy, to say the least. And might I add that she is exceedingly erotic at the same time." Morgan gasped and clapped her hands over her mouth again, but her eyes looked thrilled. "And, much to my delight, she is extremely … pleasing." Collin took a deep breath, then looked his father straight in the face. "And she is the most flexible woman that I've ever met, if I do say so myself."

Morgan and Betty gasped, looking momentarily shocked. Collin grinned from ear to ear, but Betty shot a furious look at him. Morgan's laughter caught Betty off guard.

"Yes, you certainly may say so yourself," George exclaimed, totally and completely approving. He adopted Betty's chorus: "That's my boy! I taught him well! Yes, I did!"

Chapter 8

Collin knew firsthand that his father, though he might have a great time teasing Betty about the cheesiness of being romantic, was one himself. One evening as Collin was on his way out onto the back patio to ask his mother a question, he stopped short when he heard the sound of soft music. Music on the patio was fairly common; however, this music was smoother than usual, with a lush sound that could be called nothing but romantic.

His parents listened to various types of music, both classic and current, but the song that was playing was one of their favorites. Collin had heard it played numerous times while he was growing up. Hearing some older man sing in a scratchy voice had never seemed romantic to Collin, but he had to admit that it flowed vibrantly through the speakers George had installed on the patio. His parents thought it was one the most romantic songs ever.

Collin peeked around the corner of the wall, curious. Most every evening his parents turned on the outdoor accent lighting, illuminating the pool and patio area with a dreamy effect. The result was both relaxing and picturesque.

Most nights the family ate on the patio, enjoying the beautiful evenings. George had become a grill master on the barbecue. Betty assembled the side dishes in the kitchen and brought them to the patio table just as George finished cooking on the grill. After dinner was finished and all the dishes were cleaned up, they usually each brought something outside that they could read.

On this evening, his mother sat quietly in her favorite reading chair near the outdoor fire pit, legs folded in front of her. His father walked towards her and stood a few steps away, his hand outstretched. "Shall we dance, my love?" he asked.

Betty, caught off guard by one of George's rare spontaneous yet romantic moments, smiled up at her husband, her eyes glittering. She glanced back at her book and carefully placed a bookmark in the spot where she'd stopped, then set the book down on the side table. She placed her hand in his and slowly stood in front of him. They smiled at each other as if they were two teenagers at their first high school dance. Collin could swear his mother blushed. Then they took a few steps away from Betty's chair and began to dance.

George and Betty swayed back and forth, holding each other close and giving every appearance that they didn't have a care in the world. George placed his left arm at the base of Betty's back and wrapped the other around the tops of her shoulders. He held her against his chest and rested his chin tenderly on the top of her head.

Betty's cheek pressed against George's chest, her eyes were gently shut, and her lips were formed into the softest smile Collin could remember ever having seen. It was as if she were reminiscing about their days gone past.

Halfway through the song, George lifted his chin ever so slightly so that he could place a soft kiss on the top of Betty's head. Betty's arms squeezed a bit tighter around his waist, saying nothing, expressing so much.

Collin crossed his arms and leaned against the far wall, not wanting to disturb his parents, but too caught up in the moment to leave. Sometimes Collin thought his parents' simple romantic gestures were a bit corny. In the past he had stumbled upon several little lovesick notes carrying different messages, like "I love you", "I'll miss you while you're gone", and so many more. Every time Collin found those little notes he couldn't help but roll his eyes. It just seemed to him that his parents were too old to be all mushy and lovey-dovey.

Collin had always thought that "romance" was a term that could only be used when a man was wooing a woman, something a couple did while they were dating. Once a couple was married, the romance should naturally stop and a routine life begin. He assumed there would be no more need for romance or anything of the sort.

Dating leads to marriage, marriage leads to children, having children leads to grandchildren and before you know it, life in general becomes busy and mundane. And if a person is lucky enough to fall in love with someone with whom he or she can coexist happily, then that is all there ever needed to be.

But in that moment, that very moment, witnessing his starry-eyed mother and chivalrous father holding each other with such compassion, he decided that this was the type of love that he would one day have for himself. That was the moment when Collin learned that nothing less would do.

Collin and Joey grew up in a happy home and had a wonderful childhood. As a family they enjoyed not only the playful, affectionate times, but also the occasions when there was no need to say a word to one another. Sometimes just knowing that they were together meant more than words could possibly say.

To Collin's knowledge, his parents had never had an argument. Sure, they'd had a few disagreements, but he'd never seen or heard them yell or scream at each other. They believed, and taught their sons, that most disagreements could be sorted out by simply listening to each other's opinions. And they were consistently interested in each other's opinions. The pros and cons for each issue were discussed rationally, and with respect. Collin thought his parents were unusual in that way, since he'd witnessed a lot of relationships which weren't nearly as open and understanding.

Collin vowed that he would have a marriage like the one his parents had. They always seemed happy, and always had something to talk about. It could be anything from the local news, books or something as trivial as a new game one of them found on the internet to play, but there was always something for them to share.

The only thing that could possibly make his parents any happier than they already were would be to have grandchildren. Although Collin and Joey had no immediate plans of having children, Collin knew that when they did, their children would be pampered and spoiled rotten - in a good way.

Collin listened to the song come to an end and watched his father place his fingertips on his mother's cheek. She looked up at him as if there were no one else on earth but the two of them. George bent down slightly so he could give her a soft kiss on her lips. They held each other's gaze for a moment longer, then they smiled.

All at once their romantic interlude was over and they were back to their playful selves. Betty grabbed George by the backside and growled something that sounded suspiciously like "hubba hubba!" while a sly little grin crossed her face. George grinned from ear to ear and whispered something into Betty's ear. She giggled like a school girl.

Collin rolled his eyes. He and Joey had, for as long as he could remember, learned to endure their parents' endless flirtations. It always felt odd, and a little uncomfortable, to witness their parents flirting with one another. Not that they ever did anything that was inappropriate in any way. It was just that it seemed weird. Weren't they too old to flirt?

Nevertheless, his parents were undeniably their own best friends. If something ever happened to one of them, the other would surely die of loneliness and a broken heart. He wasn't even sure one could actually live without the other.

Chapter 9

May 2011

What's that damn noise?

Collin lay in bed, rocking gently on his fishing boat, his mouth tasting like the inside of an old sock. Keeping his eyes squeezed safely shut against the possibility of bright sunshine, he stretched out one arm as he recognized the irritating beep of the alarm clock. His hand waved and fumbled around, trying to locate the snooze button, knocking over beer cans as he searched. Half a dozen cans crashed onto the floor next to his bed, then rolled around noisily while he continued to hunt for the snooze button.

Just ten more minutes. That's all I need. Within moments, the sounds of the water had rocked him back into a deep, peaceful sleep.

"Are you going to get up today?" A voice called from above. It was Joey, waking Collin in the most annoying manner, as he did every day.

"Leave me alone," Collin grumbled, curling an extra pillow tightly under his arms.

"The sun is shining, the birds are chirping, and you're still asleep at two in the afternoon!" Joey practically sang. He moved around as loudly as he could, banging boxes and pots, stomping heavily on deck.

Collin rolled over onto his back, arm slung over his eyes. "What day is it?" he managed.

"What day is it? It's Mom's and Dad's anniversary," Joey stated flatly. Collin heard his brother's footsteps as they stepped off the boat.

Anniversary? What in the world was Joey talking about? Mom and Dad's anniversary? Mom and Dad were married in June, and right now it was only the middle of May. Damn, Joey. Let me sleep!

Then it all came back like a recurring nightmare, and Collin felt as if someone had just punched him, knocked the wind out of his lungs. Today was indeed his parents' anniversary. The anniversary of their deaths. George and Betty had been killed on Joey's graduation day, one year ago today.

The police report had stated that the car explosion was a freak accident. A leaking fuel line, to be more precise.

Collin had never forgiven himself for that freak accident. The car had belonged to him. It should have been he who had died in that explosion. But Collin hadn't been the one to turn the key in the ignition. That had been George. The car exploded while it stood in the driveway of their home, and their parents were killed instantly while Collin had been safe in their home.

Over the next year, Collin took up drinking, not wanting to do much of anything. His guilt over knowing that he should have been the one that was killed, not his parents, took over his soul.

As his penance, Collin was given a huge responsibility: taking care of Joey. Although Joey was a year out of high school, he still needed looking after, and Collin wasn't doing a very good job at it.

* * *

Morgan

It had been nearly a year since George and Betty died. Yet Morgan continued to visit Collin and Joey every day. On her days off work she did some shopping for them and helped Joey clean the house. Every evening Morgan either cooked dinner or ordered take-out. Then she and Joey ate on the back patio. Sometimes they talked for hours.

"I still can't believe they're gone," Joey said one night. "That it's been almost an entire year. It feels like another lifetime."

They were eating pizza and listening to the shushing of the ocean. It was comforting to know that at least that one thing would never change.

"Me, either," Morgan said.

"Is Collin going to eat tonight?"

Morgan shook her head and stared out over the ocean. "No. He said he wasn't hungry," she replied vaguely. That wasn't a surprise. Collin rarely ate anymore. He had lost so much weight during the past year that his clothes hung loose and looked oversized.

"What's on your mind, Morgan?" Joey asked gently.

She looked at him for moment, hesitating as if she weren't sure how much to share. She wasn't used to burdening him because she'd known him as a kid before. But now he was a man. He'd been forced to become one all on his own. He tried to encourage her with a nod.

"It's just that … " she said, then hesitated before going on. When she did, her words came slowly and her eyes drifted towards Collin's boat. "It's hard to talk to him now."

"Yeah, I know," Joey said, trying to inject a little humor into the mood. "He hardly talks to me, but then again I love to aggravate him. I'm pretty loud in the mornings, and I do it on purpose. If he's still on his boat when I'm ready to leave, I do my best to wake him up, banging and yelling until he can't help but hear me. It usually pisses him off enough to at least yell a few choice words at me. I know it's not much, but at least he's saying something. It's better than nothing, I suppose."

"I've tried talking to him, Joey," Morgan said, bringing her attention back to the table. "I understand he doesn't want to talk about what happened. If I bring it up, he only gets angry. Yesterday he told me to mind my own business and ignored me until I left, and I hadn't even asked him about that in particular. I mean, he doesn't even want to hear about my day or the news or our friends, or talk about anything."

"I'm sorry Morgan," Joey said. "He's the same with me."

Morgan gazed back at Collin's boat. "I miss our talks. We used to be so close. We'd talk all the time, about anything and everything, sometimes staying up all night just talking. We had big plans. The happy Collin I once knew no longer exists, and I really miss him. I want to hold him, reassure him, but he hasn't touched me since the accident. No kisses, no hugs, no nothing. We would've been married by now, you know? I bet you didn't know we were saving to buy a house."

Joey didn't say anything. He felt sorry for Morgan because she was obviously trying so hard. And for what?

"Deep down I know it's not going to happen anymore. That part of my life will never happen," Morgan said, then quickly wiped a stray tear from her cheek. "It breaks my heart to see Collin like this. I keep hoping that he'll snap out of it, but he barely talks to me. And when he does talk, it's like he's not really there.

"Yeah, he ignores the calls from the fishing tourists, too. He doesn't want to talk to anyone or do anything," Joey said.

"I haven't seen Collin laugh or smile in almost a year. I've slowly watched his depression progress into something deeper than I could ever have imagined. It's not healthy," Morgan said, twisting the napkin between her fingers. "He started drinking to help ease the pain. That's what he said, anyway. It's one of the worst excuses I've ever heard. But I know better. I'm a nurse. I've seen a lot of things. He needs some counseling to overcome this grief, but he refuses to talk about doing that."

"I could try to talk to him," Joey said. "Maybe if I make him mad enough, he'd see one." Joey tried to laugh to ease the seriousness of the conversation, but it fell flat.

It bothered Joey seeing his brother this way. Collin looked awful lately with his hair uncombed and his face unshaven. Joey had actually boarded his boat that morning and it stunk. He wasn't sure if the smell came from all the garbage strewn around the deck, or if it came from Collin. Crushed beer cans lay scattered around and the trash that overflowed with molding food. Joey thought about throwing his brother overboard, since Collin obviously wasn't showering.

"Collin's depression is getting to me," Morgan admitted, her words almost a whisper. "I need to make a decision or I'll be the one needing to seek counseling."

"What do you mean?"

"I worry about Collin so much that it's affecting my job. My supervisor suggested that I should take some time off work, but I refused because if I did, I know I'd just be here, looking after Collin. And all he does is drink and sleep, so what's the point?"

"What decision are you talking about?" Joey asked.

"I don't think Collin wants me to come around anymore. When he does notice me, it's like he doesn't care if I stay or go. I feel like I'm in the way," Morgan said softly.

Joey sat quietly, waiting. He knew what she was about to say, and it hurt, thinking of what Collin had done to her. She'd been taking care of him and Collin for nearly a year, and Joey had wondered why she'd stuck around so long. Collin had destroyed his relationship with Morgan, and Joey wondered if Collin even cared. Or if he even knew.

Morgan dropped her head into her hands and rubbed her fingers against her head, as if trying to ease the tension. "He shrugs away when I try to touch his arm or brush the hair out of his eyes. He doesn't even want me to touch him! I thought I was strong enough to handle all of this. I thought I could help Collin through this and get us back to the way things were. But I was wrong."

"It's not your fault, Morgan," Joey said.

"I don't think Collin would even know if I broke off our engagement, you know? Deep down I want to believe he still loves me, but his depression has taken over his life. I don't know him anymore," Morgan said, then gave up and started to cry.

Joey had never been good with crying women, and it upset him to see Morgan do it. He felt useless. He handed her a napkin and didn't say a word.

Morgan wiped her tears and tried to speak calmly. "I love Collin with all my heart, but I have no other choice. I have to end our relationship. The Collin I once knew no longer exists. Maybe one day he'll find his way back to me, maybe not. I'm going to miss him, and it'll be hard. That's for sure. But he can't … he can't ever say I didn't try."

"No, he can't," Joey said quietly.

Morgan helped Joey clean up the dinner dishes, then gave Joey a hug.

"Joey, I hate to leave you like this. You've become like a brother to me. But I can't stay, and I think you know that."

"I do. But I'll miss you, Morgan. He'll never know how good he had it or how badly he wrecked it."

She gave him a crooked smile and hugged him again. Tears rolled down her face, wetting his own cheeks.

"I will always love him," Morgan told him, her voice muffled in his shoulder. "But he's dragging me down with him. I can't live like this anymore."

Eventually she let go. She touched Joey's cheek with her fingertips and looked him in the eyes, then took a deep breath before going on. "I'm sorry, Joey. I just can't do this anymore. Goodbye. Take care of yourself."

Morgan turned, wiping the tears from her face with her fingers. She didn't look back as she headed through the house and toward her car. Joey read her posture, her steps, and knew there was nothing casual in the way she left. She walked that way, tall and without any hesitation, because she was afraid she would change her mind and stay. But she got in her car and drove away. And never came back.

Sometimes Joey wondered if Collin even knew Morgan had gone.

Chapter 10

Collin stopped all fishing excursions. He became reclusive, irritable and withdrawn, isolating himself for long periods at a time. A few days, a week, it didn't matter to Collin. Time meant nothing. He just didn't care about anything anymore.

Joey decided not to go to college. He told Collin he had decided to wait, not that Collin cared at all. Joey told him he just needed a little more time to sort things out before moving forward with his education.

In truth, Joey wanted to make sure Collin was okay. Yes, Collin was the one who was supposed to take care of Joey, but it had ended up being the other way around. After Morgan left, it was up to Joey to take care of Collin. There was no way Joey could abandon his brother and go off to college. Maybe he could go to college when Collin was back to his old self. But until then, Joey wasn't going, no matter how long it took.

Collin never pushed the college issue. He knew Joey was right. He could attend college when he was good and ready. Collin didn't know Joey's real reason. He thought the trauma had left Joey confused and angry, preventing him from moving on. Collin even wondered if Joey blamed himself for their parents' death because it was because of Joey's high school graduation that they were driving in the first place. If Joey hadn't been graduating, they wouldn't have died.

When Collin was lucid, he was consumed by thoughts of that dreadful day. If only his dad had purchased the battery he needed for their car. If only Collin had taken the time to have his own vehicle maintained and serviced. If only Joey's graduation had been on a different day. If only this and if only that ... if only he could turn back time, things would be different.

Joey handled the death of his parents far better than Collin did. He woke up early every morning, chipper as usual. Though he'd postponed entry, he was still eager to someday head to college, and left the house every day to go to the library. He studied as if it were a job, reading and keeping up with the latest research books and magazines. When the day came for college, Joey promised himself that he would be more than ready.

Joey also had a social life. He occasionally even went on a few dates. He took care of the house and did the little things that needed to be done. Like their father, Joey wasn't able to sit still for long. He had to be doing something constantly, whatever that might be.

Joey was sitting at the kitchen table when Collin stumbled through the back door of the house, holding his head. He was still spending most of his time on his boat, which was fine with Joey. "Where's the Tylenol? I have a headache."

Collin always had a headache. Every day, as a matter of fact. Joey sighed. He was flipping through a new book on coral reefs he'd just picked up the other day. "It's on the shelf. Exactly where you left it yesterday." Joey looked up, recognized the familiar, rumpled look on his brother's face and sighed again. He decided to try anyway. "Are you going to work on the yacht today? It's going to be a great day. We could go get some more supplies if you need, and I'd be glad to help."

"One day," Morgan had said, and Joey has never forgotten those words. Yes, my brother. One day you will wake up again.

"No, not today," Collin mumbled. He filled a glass with water, preparing to take his first dose of Tylenol for the day. "I have other things to do."

Joey slammed his fist on the table, finally losing patience. "You know what, Collin? You always have other things to do! But here's the thing. I don't see you doing anything! Nothing! All you do is drink. You never used to drink. And I'm sick of it. I'm sick of your whole self-serving attitude, the whole poor me thing you're doing!

They were my parents too, you know!" Joey shouted.

Collin winced and placed a hand on his forehead.

Joey was on a roll and decided to keep on going. "You don't see me moping around, feeling sorry for myself. Grow up, man. You're twenty-five years old, for Christ's sake! I'm only nineteen and I know you're acting like a baby."

Joey stood up, gaining momentum. He moved closer to Collin and jabbed one finger into his brother's chest. "You're supposed to be the adult, Collin. But in case you haven't noticed, I'm the one taking care of you. What would Mom and Dad say if they could see you now?"

"Look, you little bastard!" Collin roared, and Joey noticed a vein pressing against his brother's forehead. He didn't recall that being there before. In fact, he didn't remember even seeing so much red in Collin's face until recently. "You don't have to take care of me! I'm doing just fine!" Collin turned away, hacking until his face went red.

Chapter 11

Collin's health had become a priority for Joey. It hurt him to look at his older brother these days. He was always sleeping, his skin seemed blotchy, almost puffy. He was always weak, tired and, though Joey knew Collin would hate the very idea of it, he seemed almost fragile.

Collin was broken. He needed help, but Joey knew he would never ask for it. Was he sick with something other than grief and guilt? Joey didn't know how to tell. Collin wouldn't have told Joey anything anyway.

Because he didn't know what else to do about it, Joey made sure the house was stocked with different over-the-counter medicines so Collin would have them just in case. He also filled the fridge and cabinets with healthy food so there'd be no danger of Collin eating the wrong things. He couldn't think of what other steps to take.

Collin never made mention of any of it, nor did he acknowledge that Joey was now taking care of the household. But Joey knew Collin ate some of the food. He also knew Collin came in the house when he was gone. Somehow that was comforting. Collin might not want to talk to anyone, but at least Joey knew he wasn't lying around in bed all day. He wanted to make sure this kind of progress continued, so he always left the house vacant for at least part of the day, every day. That was another reason he headed out to the library each day, besides wanting to hang with some of his friends.

But this morning Joey'd had just about enough. He'd done everything he could, and he'd been more patient than anyone could have expected him to be. He wanted to make a point this morning, whether Collin's head was up for it or not. He had to let off some steam or he might explode.

"Oh, yeah," he said with a sneer, taunting him. At least if he could get a rise out of Collin he'd feel more alive. He hadn't backed off when Collin had yelled, and there was no way he was going to now. "You sure do look like you're doing fine. Do you remember what you promised me? You said you were going to fix up the yacht. You said you were going to take me away, that you and I were going to get out of this place and sail around the world. Forget everything that had happened and be happy, out on the water, just you and me. That's what you said."

Joey's hands tightened into fists. He wanted to shake some sort of sense back into Collin. "Were you lying to me? Come on, you idiot. It's been a year. An entire year. I've been waiting a year! Is that day ever going to come? Answer me, you fucking drunk!"

The room was quiet, but to Joey it sounded as if his voice echoed forever. Adrenaline roared through his system, making his hands shake as he stared down his brother.

Collin didn't answer. He just stood there, looking dazed. After a moment, he took a deep breath, but still looked straight ahead, past Joey. Joey could almost hear him thinking and wanted to whoop with happiness. Maybe he'd gotten through! Maybe something would happen today.

Collin's eyes focused on Joey again. When he spoke it was calm. "When it's time, I'll tell you. Then we'll leave, no looking back. We'll just go, leave everything behind. I'll tell you when it's time."

Joey stared at him, so angry he wanted to shake his brother silly. "Sounds like a bunch of bullshit to me!" he shouted. He headed towards the front door, grabbing his wallet from the hall table as he went. He glared back over his shoulder at Collin. "I'm going to get the damn mail. Do me a favor, would you, brother?" he said mockingly. "Try to pull yourself together. And do me another one. Take a shower. You smell like a fucking brewery!"

Joey stormed out, slamming the door behind him so hard that the picture frames rattled on the wall.

Collin stared down the empty hallway, exhaling through loose lips. He felt worn down as thin as he could go.

71

"I think that went rather well," Collin mumbled to himself, then turned away.

* * *

"Damn it! What am I doing wasting my time here? He's nothing but a self-pitying, self-centered jackass," Joey said to himself.

He shoved his hands into the front pockets of his shorts and stared at the ground, kicking every stone he saw as he walked down the long driveway toward the mailbox. He didn't expect there to be any mail. He just needed to get a bit of fresh air. The mail was an excuse to walk out and gain a little self-control before he ended up strangling his miserable waste of a brother.

Dad would've kept the driveway in better shape than this. Joey leaned down and grabbed a rock that fit neatly into the palm of his hand, and chucked it ahead of him. He imagined his dad sweeping up, checking to make sure nothing needed fixing.

Collin wasn't the only one grieving. Joey thought of his parents every day. He just wasn't able to share any of that with Collin. He had to be the strong one. If Dad were here, Collin wouldn't have turned into a senseless drunk. If Mom were here, she would have made sure he'd showered, at least.

"Joey! Hey! Joey!"

Joey stopped abruptly and looked up the road, narrowing his gaze at the classic 1963 blue Chevrolet Low-rider which was slowing down and finally coming to a stop at the end of Joey's driveway. Now that was a nice ride.

"Hey guys," Joey said, walking casually towards the car. It was a bit of a stretch to paste on a smile after his recent run-in with Collin, but he managed. Talking with his friends always helped take his mind off the less pleasant aspects of his life, including his brother's idiocy and sadly lacking sense of responsibility. Joey grinned at the guys, feeling a welcome surge of energy. No way he was going to allow Collin to ruin his day.

Chapter 12

Joey was right, as usual. Collin sighed, thinking about it. He hated the fact that his little brother was so much stronger than he was. He lifted his forearm to his nose and sniffed. Joey was right about that, too. He did smell like a brewery. Taking a hot shower sounded like a good idea. He stretched, reaching towards the ceiling with a loud groan, then scratched his head. Yup. Shampoo would be good, too. Maybe even a shave.

Today might even be a good day to work on the yacht, he thought. If nothing else, at least it would get Joey off his back for a while. He started up the coffee pot and walked towards the bathroom. On his way down the hall, he glanced out the large by window in the living room. It was a pretty day. The water sparkled with invitation.

Joey stood at the end of their driveway, talking to a few of his friends. They'd pulled up in a classic blue car and Joey was leaning in the passenger window.

Collin yawned again, then forced his aching body to continue towards the bathroom. "Jeez," he thought. "I just woke up and I already need a nap."

The hot water felt incredible, pulsating on his tired skin like a massage. He leaned his head against the back of the shower wall, letting the water do its magic. He was tempted to stay like that all day.

"Nope," he said out loud. "Gotta get my butt in gear today." Shower and a quick shave. That should do it.

"Your coffee is ready!" Collin heard Joey yell, but he didn't reply. He rubbed the condensation off the bathroom mirror and stared at his reflection, combing his fingers through his wet hair. He was badly in need of a haircut.

"Did you hear me?" Joey demanded from outside the bathroom door. Collin swung open the door and walked out, wearing a towel wrapped around his waist. He was rubbing a smaller towel vigorously over his head.

Collin looked away when Joey grinned, happy at the sight of Collin clean and doing something. Collin didn't want to see that expression on his brother's face. He knew he'd let him down, but wasn't about to take ownership of that. Not yet.

He didn't bother answering Joey's stupid question. In fact he made a point of ignoring him. Of course he'd heard him. Who in the entire neighborhood hadn't? Joey spoke so loud all the time it was amazing he wasn't deaf.

Collin was well aware of what Joey was up to. He was doing everything he could do to get on Collin's last nerve, get some kind of reaction out of him. Joey usually did a fine job at that.

"What's with all the packages that you keep getting?" Joey asked. "What's going on?" Collin glanced at him, then looked away when he saw the sarcasm in his brother's expression. "You're always getting packages in the mail. Oh, look! There goes the FedEx truck! Hmm. I wonder if he'll be stopping here." For a second, Collin almost smiled. His parents would have been proud of Joey's sarcasm. It was definitely shining through today.

Collin continued to ignore him. He grabbed a coffee mug and placed it gently on the counter, then opened the fridge, searching for the milk.

But Joey had no intention of stopping. He was peering out the window, shaking his head. "Damn, he didn't stop! Well, don't feel too bad. You could always hope for the UPS man. I'm sure he'll be coming down the road soon. Then you can go out and sign for whatever it is." Joey clicked his tongue as if he were disappointed. "It sure is a sad day when you don't get any packages delivered, huh? It's such a shame."

Joey faked a broad, salesman's smile, then winked at Collin. He tapped his fingers on the table just to irritate him even more.

Collin snapped. "It's none of your business, you nosey little shit! You'll know when I want you to know."

"Whatever!" Joey retorted, dropping the sarcasm like a hot potato. "You know what? I'm sick of this. I'm going to the library. Try to stay sober today, will you?"

Joey grabbed his keys and left, slamming the door for the second time that morning.

"How much longer is this going to go on?" Joey asked out loud, stomping towards his car. "I'm not sure how much more of this I can handle. I'm nineteen years old for Christ's sake! I'm only nineteen years old!" He reached for the door handle, then stopped, resting his elbows on the roof of the car. He dropped his forehead onto his arms when tears flooded his eyes.

What was he going to do? All he had left in this world was Collin. Collin. Damn you, Collin.

Joey had a lot of friends, but they weren't family. And even though Joey saw Collin every day, interacted with him in whatever manner, he missed his brother. This Collin was nothing like the brother he used to have. That brother used to talk with him about school or girls or anything else that was on his mind. That brother used to take him out fishing every weekend.

That brother was his best friend, and he used to love him. The same brother was now full of empty promises.

"God, Collin. Enough already," he said through his tears. "Oh, Mom. I wish you and Dad were here. I miss you both so much."

Joey wiped an arm across his eyes and got into his car, gripping the steering wheel hard enough that his knuckles turned white. He sat for a minute without turning on the engine, feeling more bitter by the moment.

"The jerk managed to ruin my day after all," he thought. "No big surprise." He turned the key and put the car in gear, but wasn't soothed by the familiar purr of his engine.

* * *

Collin poured a second cup of coffee and sat at the kitchen table, sipping. He needed to cool down after having survived the latest dramatic encounter with Joey. Would his lectures never end?

He decided to head down to the yacht and do a few things on it that day. But he wanted to do it by himself, without his nagging little brother.

The packages to which Joey had so gently referred were piling up in the general living area of the yacht. It was well past time that he put everything away. Collin hadn't ordered any new items over the past few weeks, since he'd figured these last packages should be enough. Now that they were all here he'd put them in their right places. Just like his dad used to do with his tools.

Collin, like his mom, was a planner. He found it satisfying to be prepared for whatever might come and always stockpiled provisions just in case. He pulled out his pocket knife and slit open the packages one by one. Then he began to unpack the individual items, placing each of them in their rightful place, and as he did so, he felt life around him shift gradually into place as well.

Throughout high school, Joey had rarely been involved with the cleaning or repair of the yacht. He showed little interest and hardly stepped foot aboard, always claiming he had too much studying to do. Maybe that was true, since he basically lived at the library.

Collin snorted. Joey still lived at the library. He hadn't boarded the yacht since the death of their parents. Collin paused, wondering. For Joey to offer to help Collin with the yacht was out of the ordinary.

"Something must have changed," Collin thought, then shrugged and got back to work.

Collin's original plan had been to rebuild, then sell the yacht at a higher price when the market went up. That way he'd make a profit. However, Collin had decided not to sell it. However painful they were to remember, the yacht was filled with wonderful memories of his parents. Selling the yacht would feel like selling their home, which he hadn't even considered doing. He just couldn't do it. The memories were worth more to him than any profit that might be made by selling the yacht.

Collin was like his mother Betty in many ways. He always thought of the future. He planned what needed to be done and what items needed to be purchased. Joey had no idea what the packages were for or what they contained. But the idea that he had to plan and be prepared for anything was continuously on Collin's mind.

Collin's yacht did not need any further repairs. It was in perfect shape and in the best possible mechanical running condition. It was clean and perfect, just as it had been when his parents had died. Collin made sure to keep everything dusted and in their proper places. His mother would have been proud.

Chapter 13

Despite everything his family believed, Collin had stopped taking visiting tourists on fishing excursions years ago. But he did have a business, and he was busy. And he was making a boatload of money.

Collin had a secret activity that no one else knew about. Two or three times a week Collin helped transport Cubans from Cuba to Florida. Cuba was approximately ninety miles from Key West. That meant Key West was even closer to Cuba than it was to Miami. Instead of shuttling tourists around, Collin transported Cubans.

Collin's large fishing boat was perfect for the task. She was strong enough to withstand rough sea weather and large enough to easily hold ten people, but Collin never transported more than five Cubans at a time. Collin was paid five hundred dollars for each person that he transported, which meant he could make anywhere from fifty-five hundred to seventy-five hundred dollars per week. That, in anybody's opinion, was a pretty good chunk of change. That was more than what some people could earn in a six months working an average minimum wage job.

Because of his earlier fishing excursions, Collin was very knowledgeable about the waters in the Straits of Florida. He knew the current, where to fish and where not to fish. He also knew not to cross, come too close, or cross over the invisible dividing line separating the United States from Cuban waters.

Five years before the death of his parents, Collin had been on a fishing excursion by himself, testing out his new fish finder. He'd been enjoying the water and relaxing, thinking about nothing much, when another large fishing boat came about and slowly headed towards Collin's boat. Thinking nothing of it, since the Straits of Florida were widely known for deep sea fishing and scuba diving, Collin went back to watching his fishing poles.

The unknown boat came closer to Collin's boat and finally stopped at a safe distance, about fifty feet away. A young Cuban man, maybe a bit older than Collin, waved his arms and shouted, "Ahoy there!"

The young Cuban man, Adelio, was friendly and interesting, and he spoke English very well. Fortunately, Collin knew a little Spanish as well, so the two men understood each other fairly easily. Before long Collin found himself having a detailed conversation with the man. Adelio came right out and asked Collin if he might be interested in becoming a business partner with him. He explained the need for human transportation, helping Cubans get safely to America.

"Thousands of men, women and children have perished in the water. They are so desperate to escape Cuba that they are willing to try to float ninety miles on an inner tube or a shabby little raft. Those who illegally left Cuba on homemade rafts are known as 'Balseros'". Adelio hung his head and continued. "They did not have fear of the many sea creatures brushing up against them, such as sharks, because they would spread themselves with old motor oil to keep the creatures away. This was a trick they learned from fishermen." A quick smile crossed Adelio's face, then disappeared.

"Many Cubans are swindled and captured by human traffickers. The captured Cubans are made to do forced labor or are pressured into sex slavery because they feel they have no other option."

Collin had heard this before, the stories of how many Cubans, not knowing how to make a new life in another country, believed the lies that the human traffickers told them. The traffickers promised them a new life and a different kind of work, but through these lies the Cubans are pulled into a web of deception and deceit. They end up with something else, something far worse than what they had been running from.

"I've heard about these things," Collin told him.

Collin couldn't help but feel that Adelio's helping his people get to America was personal somehow. Why else wouldn't Adelio just go to America himself?

Collin sensed that Adelio was an intelligent man, but he seemed to be taking it upon himself to help as many people as he could. For a man to deliberately place himself in a dangerous situation in order to help others that he didn't know, well, to Collin's mind, that didn't even come close to rational thinking. Especially when it meant the man could possibly get killed.

On the other hand, thousands of people join the military, putting themselves in harm's way. Many of them die for their country and for people they don't know. But that was different, wasn't it?

"You sound like this is something very personal to you, Adelio. I mean, more than just helping your people."

"Oh, it is, my friend. I shall tell you my story."

Chapter 14

When Adelio was only ten years old, he had helped his father build a small wooden raft and an ore. All the time they were building their raft, Adelio's father told him stories about the free world, America.

"Sailing to freedom," his father would say.

The reason they were building a raft was because it had the advantage of not being easily detected by radar. He had to be very careful. Because he was leaving Cuba without permission, he feared reprisals against his family and friends.

While Adelio and his father prepared the raft for his illegal exit, his father reluctantly explained that the journey was extremely dangerous. It was true that on some summer days, when there was a stiff wind from the south, crossing the straits could be relatively easy. If the prevailing winds blew in the direction of the Gulf Stream, they could propel a raft from the north coast of Cuba all the way to the Florida Keys. The current, at times, could be like a warm river which coursed northeastward along a route. When this happened it was quite convenient for a Cuban refugee.

But for the most part, the trip could be deadly. Adelio's father told his son that only about half of those who embark on the crossing actually make it to Florida. The others are either caught by Cuban authorities or they drown. As soon as a raft leaves Cuba, it enters waters that are three thousand, three hundred and ninety feet deep. On rough summer days and throughout the winter, when the wind and sea currents clash, the seas can get "ungodly high". During those times, the waves rise so high they are like mountains.

Adelio's father didn't want to tell him everything, but knew he had to be honest with his son. So he told him how nature can sometimes be a rafter's best accomplice, but rarely. Adelio almost couldn't listen when his father told him that over the years, many rafts had been found floating either empty or cradling a dead, sunburned body.

But the family was so desperate for a different life from the one they led in Cuba that they, and so many others, were willing to attempt this almost impossible voyage.

Adelio's father's raft was hidden off the shoreline, camouflaged within the heavy brush where he and Adelio often went fishing. It had been outfitted with water, nets, and extra clothes to keep him safe from the harsh elements.

Adelio remembered clearly the day his father was to leave for America. He had given his son a long, tight hug, then told him to be a good boy. He promised that when it was time, he would send for both Adelio and his mother. By then it would be legal for them to come to live with him in America.

Adelio remembered his mother crying so hard she was almost unable to speak. She handed her husband a sack which contained the bare necessities for his voyage. The sack was heavy - Adelio could see that from the way his father slumped a bit after slinging the bag over one shoulder. They had worked together compiling this little bundle, filling it with a can of old motor oil from a mechanic they knew, an old pair of binoculars, an old wind-up watch, two boiled chickens, a few cans of evaporated milk, and some rice and beans.

His father reached into his pocket, pulled out a knife and a compass, needing to assure himself that he had them both packed away. Nodding with satisfaction, he dropped them back into his pocket, then gave it a little tap for luck.

He held Adelio's weeping mother tightly against him, kissing her and muttering something meant to reassure her into her ear. It didn't seem to be working, though Adelio could see she was trying to contain herself, if only for him. His father stepped away from her at last, patted Adelio on the head, then turned to leave.

When he was only a few steps away from the door, Adelio's

father turned back towards Adelio. He knelt in front of his son and removed the cross necklace which had always hung around his neck. This he draped around Adelio's neck. He told his son that the cross had been given to him by his father and it would keep Adelio safe.

"But Father, you need it to keep yourself safe," the little Adelio said.

His father shook his head. "I shall be fine. I need you to be safe and take care of your mother. Can you do that for me?"

Adelio nodded somberly and felt his mother's fingers squeeze his shoulders from behind. He held the cross in his fingers and examined it carefully. In the middle was a small red gem, which shimmered beautifully in the dim lamplight. Inscribed on the back of the cross was his family name.

His father patted his head again, then nodded slightly. He got to his feet, turned to the door, and walked away without another word. That was in the year 1992.

Five years later, when Adelio was fifteen years old, his mother got sick. They couldn't afford the proper medicines to help her survive the illness, and she died while Adelio sat at her bedside. Ironically, Adelio's father had been a doctor, and had he remained with them in Cuba, he might have been able to heal her. But being a doctor in Cuba meant very little. In their country, a taxi driver made more money than a doctor.

Adelio had received no word from his father in five years.

By then, Adelio was old enough to work and take care of himself. Now that he wasn't responsible for his mother anymore, he decided to start a new life.

That was what had brought him here, to the side of Collin's boat. It had been fifteen years since his father's departure, and Adelio still had not heard from him. He feared the worst, believing his father had probably died while "sailing to freedom". Either that, or he had been captured and enslaved by the traffickers. Adelio didn't know which would have been the better option.

Adelio told Collin he had dedicated his life to the memory of his father. And the way he did this was by helping Cubans find freedom and happiness in America. He wanted to safely transport them while keeping them out of the hands of human traffickers.

"When someone is told that they can get free transportation to America and when they get there they might even be given a job, they will most likely jump at such a generous offer. They are so desperate to get a job and money that they will do anything. The fall of the economy and lack of jobs has made people eager for any opportunity at a better life." Adelio looked Collin straight in the eye. "Wouldn't you do the same for your family?"

Collin nodded warily.

"However, once the so-called destination is reached, the traffickers tell the Cubans that they have to work for the transporters in order to pay off the cost of travel. Being gullible and thinking that this makes sense, they agree to work off the cost. Then the traffickers pay little to nothing and make it impossible for the workers to pay off their debt. This way, the citizens of Cuba fall into the trap of human trafficking and are stuck in a vicious cycle of hardship and poverty for the rest of their lives."

Collin was torn. It sounded dangerous, and from everything he'd read, it was highly illegal. And yet if he got involved, he would be helping these people. Keeping them safe and offering them a new life. Not only that, but he could make a lot of money while he was doing it.

So maybe human trafficking had an upside: it brought together the new business arrangement between Collin and Adelio. The two men shook hands and discussed contact arrangements over the internet, as well as dates, times, meeting points and so on.

Chapter 15

Over the next little while, Collin learned a great deal from his new friend. Adelio told him that under the current "Wet-foot, Dry-foot" policy, Cubans who reach American soil were generally allowed to remain in the United States, while those stopped at sea were sent home. That made the successful travelers more likely to contact the American government upon their arrival, unlike other illegal immigrants who tended to hide from law enforcement.

Adelio brought the Cubans to Collin, who then transported them to U.S. soil. The two were good partners and trusted each other implicitly.

The job was easy for Collin because he felt good about what he was doing. Collin was a compassionate man and was sympathetic to the citizens of Cuba. He believed that Adelio and he were doing a wonderful thing, helping people to freedom and out of poverty. Most of the refugees they transported were young, and all desired a better way of life. They wanted to get established in America and eventually try to bring the rest of their families over legally.

Collin never felt threatened by anyone he transported. In fact most of the time the people that boarded his fishing boat did nothing at all but nod gratefully at him, and they were more than willing to sit wherever Collin indicated. Most never uttered a sound throughout the entire trip. Collin invested some of his own money every time, providing each person with their own backpack. The pack was filled with non-perishable food, water, and a map so that they had at least that much when they arrived in the new country. Each backpack also contained an envelope containing one hundred dollars.

The Cubans paid Adelio, and when Collin picked up the passengers halfway through the Straits of Florida, he was given an envelope by Adelio, paying him for that evening's work. The rendezvous always took place in the late evenings. Collin was paid in American money, which seemed a little curious, but it was something Collin never asked about.

He also never asked Adelio how much the Cubans actually paid for the transportation. Sometimes he wondered if Adelio kept half the money, but knowing Adelio as he did, that didn't feel right. For some reason, Collin had a feeling Adelio gave most of the money to Collin, if not all of it.

An online ad informed Collin of the days for the exchange, as well as the location. The locations were never spelled out, just in case the ads were intercepted, but Collin knew where to go. They had arranged specific pickup locations and given them each a specific letter name. The letter A appearing at the end of the online ad would mean Collin was supposed to go to one particular location. The letters B, C and D directed him to different spots.

If there were ever any changes, another online ad would be placed. Collin checked the online listings every morning at a certain time, making sure he knew exactly when and if a meeting was going to take place.

They ran a tight little business, helping others, helping themselves, and Collin really didn't see any problems with it.

Chapter 16

Cuban Departure Day 1

My name is Gavin. Today I leave Cuba. Cuba is the only home I have ever known. I left just after midnight with only stars for light. It was very dark because I had to leave when no one could see.

I journey across the ocean, floating to America and to my freedom. It should only take four days or so to cross the water. Six days at the most.

I leave without permission from my government, and I leave without my family and my friends. Some call this an illegal exit. Only my wife and son know of my leaving. I could not take the risk of others knowing, no matter how close they are to me. After it is discovered that I am gone, all of them will be put under surveillance and interrogated by the Cuban government. Even those that do not know of my leaving. I pray for them all.

I am a doctor, but the pay is not what it should be. I try very hard, but I must be able to provide for my family, and we can no longer live a decent life in Cuba. Some people would think me a foolish man for taking this risk. I believe it is not I who am the fool. The fools are the ones who believe Cuba will get better. They wait forever, hoping for a change, but this is not the answer.

Yes, I am afraid of this journey. But I would rather die trying than continue to live in poverty in Cuba.

I built a makeshift raft, and I am actually quite proud of its design. The raft is slightly larger than I am, and held together with twine. By building it that way there is less to be detected and it is easier to disguise. I could have made a larger raft, one I could have filled with more food and water, but then I would have been more easily discovered. I had to take my chances with a smaller raft.

Tucked into my raft is a thin, wooden ore which is about three feet long. My plan is to paddle for as many of the days as possible. I also have a homemade compass. It was made with a magnetized needle stuck through a cork to help guide me towards America.

I hope I have enough food and water to last me for six days. I plan to eat and drink sparingly, just in case the winds or the current make my journey longer than anticipated. Everything I have to eat and drink is wrapped in plastic and tied with twine to the edges of the raft.

The weather can be unpredictable, so I am wearing a short sleeve shirt as well as a long sleeve shirt, and long shorts to protect me from the sun and harsh elements. There is no need to wear socks or shoes.

I have a small knife in my pocket as well as some used motor oil in a few small containers. These are to help fend off sharks and keep me safe. Many people have died trying to make this journey to America, and all of my people have heard the horrible stories over and over again. Some people have starved to death or drowned, and those are considered the lucky ones. The worst deaths were brought on by shark attacks.

I hope the winds and currents carry me swiftly on my journey. If the currents are in my favor my raft will be like a slingshot going towards America. But this water is treacherous with all of its strong currents and many sharks.

I pray that I make it to America. I will be at the mercy of the water. I pray a lot.

I am risking everything for the love of my family, so I can give them a better life. In Cuba everyone is poor and living meaningless lives. Work is hard to find. Despite this, I have never done anything illegal in my lifetime. Not until now.

* * *

Evening

The sun was blazing hot today. My head aches and my body feels horrible, but I am trying very hard not to get sick. I can't afford to lose any fluid by doing that. Being on the open water without proper shade is worse than I could ever have imagined.

In the afternoon I couldn't wait for the sun to set. Now the cool temperature on my burned skin is making me shiver. My teeth constantly chatter.

I never knew nighttime could be so dark. The sunset was a relief for my skin, but until the stars came out I could not see much of anything, and I am terrified of the darkness. I am happy for the light of the moon and stars. They sparkle on the water and try to cheer me. I try, but I do not feel any better.

Even now, under their twinkling lights, I am unable to see the creatures of the water, so I am afraid to go to sleep. I should have brought a flashlight but I did not have the money to buy one.

I am more thirsty than hungry and when I move, my hands shake. The heat of the day has drained my energy, but I must not drink all of my water. It needs to last longer. My hands and arms are sore because I paddled most of the day. No doubt they will be aching in the morning.

I am exhausted and want to sleep, but can only afford to take short naps. I have tied my wrist to the raft with twine just in case I fall into the water while I am sleeping. I should have built some type of edge on the sides of my raft so that I wouldn't have to worry about falling into the water while I sleep. But there is no point in pondering over what ought to have been done. What's done is done. There is no going back now.

The night is quiet. Dreadfully quiet. And the water is still. I listen for sounds of any kind, but there is nothing. I feel like I am the only person on the earth. This is not a good feeling. I'm a grown man with an education. I shouldn't be afraid. But I am.

I miss my family and wonder how they are doing. Has anyone asked about me? Does anyone of authority know that I have left?

One day gone. Only three more days to go. Maybe five. I hope my journey does not turn out to be longer than I had planned. But even if it does, I must believe I can do this. I have no other choice.

Chapter 17

Although Collin only transported two or three days a week, he took his boat out every morning and evening. His reason for doing this was to ensure that the Coast Guards didn't become suspicious. They did routine checks of the boats in American waters along the Florida Strait, looking for drug traffickers and other criminals.

Collin had been stopped a couple of times but had never had any problem. He got to know some of the guards by their surnames, which were stitched onto their uniforms, and though it could never be said that he became close friends with any of them, they were on a friendly basis with him.

"Captain Scott," a Coast Guard called. "Catch anything good today?" they would typically ask.

Collin had been blessed with a trustworthy face and had a friendly manner about him that seemed to put the Coast Guards at ease. They kept their inspections short and sweet, just the way Collin liked them. He was always prepared. His fishing gear was always displayed around the boat and he set coolers around the deck, all of which were filled with ice. That way he didn't raise any suspicious eyebrows.

It also helped that on several occasions Collin took a few of his friends out on day long fishing trips, providing them with plenty of food and drinks. He always managed to time it so his friends were having plenty of fun when the Coast Guards arrived. Some of his drunken buddies purposefully joked loud enough for the Coast Guards to hear. It was all in good fun.

Occasionally he had to demand that his friends cool it, because when they overdid it they could get extremely obnoxious. Collin never drank a drop of alcohol when he was on board, and disapproved of the way his friends teased the Coast Guards when they stopped by for a spot inspection. One time it got particularly bad and Collin had a hard time quieting everyone down. The Coast Guards hadn't looked impressed.

But after this memorable occasion, Collin noticed that the Coast Guards didn't come to his boat for inspections anymore. Instead they either radioed him to ask if he needed any assistance or simply waved as they passed. So in the end, his crazy friends actually helped.

Coast Guard Perez was a regular with the evening shift aboard the patrols. Perez stood out from the rest of the officers. He was clearly not American born and had a strong Spanish accent, though he spoke English very well. Collin figured Perez would be a great asset to the Coast Guard, in case they happened to find any Cuban refugees floating on rafts in the Florida Strait.

Despite the fact that Collin still felt he was helping people by transporting them from Cuba, he also knew that what he was doing was not only illegal, but also highly dangerous. If Collin were ever caught by the Coast Guard, he would be thrown in jail, though he sometimes wondered if the Coast Guards might show a little compassion and turn a blind eye to what he was doing. While there was a slight possibility of that, Collin knew he would never get any kind of kindness from traffickers. If he were ever caught by human traffickers, he would be killed.

In addition to the occasional day trips with his friends, Collin also took friends scuba diving a few times a week. Everything was a brilliant cover. Not even Collin's closest friends knew what he was up to. They just thought he was treating them to a fun day on the sea.

Often it was just Collin and Joey in the boat. He and Joey were as close as any brothers could be, and Collin was a typical overprotective big brother.

Even though Joey wasn't keen on the boat he loved the water as much as Collin did. Collin thought it was important that Joey know everything there was to know about the fishing boat and sonar equipment. He encouraged Joey to learn as much as possible about the ocean and boating. At times Collin wondered if Joey knew more about some things than he did, but Joey never let on.

The other person Collin spent most of his time with was Adelio. They had become friends, sometimes meeting just to fish or enjoy a conversation out on the water.

He learned that Adelio had grown up in poverty and when he had managed to find work he saved every bit of money he could. As he'd grown he'd worked two jobs and long hours. One job paid him small wages and the other job provided him food in exchange for his work. Adelio eventually saved up enough money to purchase a fishing boat. With it he started his own business of helping Cubans, like himself, find a better way of life. Now he was married and his wife was expecting their first baby.

In a way, Adelio reminded Collin of Harriet Tubman. She was the escaped slave from Maryland who had eventually become recognized as the "Moses of her people". Over ten years she put her own life at tremendous risk so that she could guide hundreds of slaves to freedom through the Underground Railroad. When Collin told Adelio that, his friend looked shy but pleased.

Over time Collin and Adelio became the best of friends. Unfortunately, their friendship was limited to whatever they could do on each other's boats. Collin thought it would be great to bring

Adelio home to meet his family and friends. He knew Adelio would enjoy himself and that he would love George's fine grilling. He thought how awesome it would be if he could take him to a ballgame with some of his other friends.

But Adelio never mentioned coming to America. Collin often wondered why he simply didn't get on Collin's boat and go to America with him. But he never asked. And Collin figured if his friend hadn't mentioned it, there was probably a good reason. He assumed it was because Adelio didn't want to leave his wife and unborn baby. Then he would be just like his father before him, when he had left his mother and Adelio. It was also probably difficult for the Cuban authorities not to notice a pregnant woman getting onto a fishing boat. And after the baby was born? Well, the sight of a woman with a baby, boarding a boat was even more obvious.

Adelio loved his country. He told Collin all the time about how beautiful it was. He raved about the architecture, the endless countryside and pristine white beaches. No. Adelio would never leave his country or his family.

But that did not keep Adelio from being curious about America. He asked Collin endless questions then sat attentively, listening in amazement to the answers. Once in awhile he'd contribute little bits of trivia that always spiked Collin's interest.

"Did you know," Adelio asked one time, "that many sailors used to wear gold earrings so that they could afford a proper burial when they died?"

Collin laughed, lifting one eyebrow with surprise. "No, I didn't know that one. That's fascinating. You sound like my mother, knowing little bits and pieces of information that no one else knows. I'll have to tell her that one."

Adelio stared at him, stunned. "I sound like your mother? What do you mean?"

This time Collin laughed at his friend's expression. "Oh, nothing, really. It's just that my mother loves to enlighten people at any given moment whether it pertains to the situation or not. Her mind is full of random pieces of information that no one would probably ever need to know. 'Tidbits' she calls them." Collin said, then chuckled, recalling some of the useless information his mother had mentioned. "Truth be known, my mom could probably write a book filled with all those tidbits."

"Like what? What other tidbits did your mother tell you?" Adelio asked, his curiosity piqued.

"Well, let's see." Collin rubbed his chin, trying to choose one instance. There were so many. "Ah," he said, remembering one. "When the clans of long ago wanted to get rid of unwanted people without killing them, they burned their houses down. That is where the expression 'to get fired' comes from."

Collin was more than willing to tell stories about his family and about his childhood for as long as Adelio asked questions, which was continuously. On days that they planned to do nothing but just hang out, Collin brought newspapers and magazines for Adelio to read. They spent a few relaxing hours just reading on the boat, but Adelio would never take any of the reading material back with him. If anyone every found them on his boat he would be in great trouble. But he was always very happy to see them. He thoroughly enjoyed reading them all.

Food was also a favorite topic of conversation.

"Since the early sixties all households in Cuba are given a monthly ration of rice, beans, cooking oil, salt, sugar and bread. Sometimes we get rations of eggs and meat, but very little. Only pregnant women, young children and the sick get milk." Adelio shrugged, giving Collin a wry smile. "We will not starve, but we often worry about our next meal. And we have to be mindful of how we take care of ourselves, because we are also rationed soap and toothpaste."

Collin was shocked. "But you have a fishing boat. You can fish as much as you want, right?"

Adelio nodded. "I've lived and worked in a fishing village for many years. I am fortunate because I supply many of the village hotels with fresh fish. I am trusted by all those in authority. I also take many tourists in the hotels out fishing. My wife works in one of the hotels in the village. Cubans are not allowed to eat any lobsters because they are considered only for the elite and the tourists. Because of what I do, my wife and I eat fish every day. We are lucky in that respect. The people that live in the city are not so lucky."

"Wow," Collin said, leaning against the back of his chair. "You know, I never imagined I had it so good. I guess none of us do. We Americans take a lot of things for granted. I'd thought about the big picture of wanting 'freedom', but not the basics, like food. For example, I think if we didn't have fast food joints, the entire country would go crazy."

"Fast food?"

"Yeah. Like McDonalds, KFC, Arby's, those things. Those are everywhere in the States. I guess you don't have those."

"No. I've never even heard of those places."

"You'd love them. You just drive up and buy a burger through a window. If you have to wait longer than five minutes it feels like forever. Amazing what we take for granted."

Adelio watched him with wide eyes. "A burger? I've never had a burger." He shook his head. "That sounds like a whole different world."

"I guess it is," Collin admitted, then frowned. "Tell me, is there anything I can bring for you the next time we meet?"

"No. No, my friend. You are already doing more than any regular man would. You have already given me so much just by helping me with these people."

Chapter 18

But the next time Collin and Adelio met up, Collin arrived with a special treat. As Adelio's boat pulled alongside, Collin cupped his hands around his mouth and called out to him.

"Adelio! I have a surprise for you!"

Adelio grinned and tied his boat to Collin's. He clambered aboard the bigger fishing boat and embraced Collin, as he always did. "How are you, my friend?"

Collin hugged him back. "Oh, it's a good day, Adelio. I've brought you something I think you're really going to like."

Adelio chuckled. "I always like what you bring. I am a lucky man to have you as my friend. What did you bring today?"

"Lunch! I brought burgers since you said you'd never had one. And fries and onion rings. I stopped in at my favorite place and picked up a few things."

Collin reached behind him and opened the cooler he had set there. He had wanted to keep things as warm as possible so the cooler was packed with heated food warmers and towels. Once he had shuffled them out of the way, he pulled out two large bags and held them up for Adelio to see. He set them on a table and opened the bags.

"Next time I will treat you to something called an Italian Beef," Collin promised.

Adelio stared into the open bags, eyes as wide as a child's on Christmas morning. The smell of burgers and fries rose from the bags and Collin thought he could practically see Adelio salivating. When Adelio looked back up at him, Collin was surprised to see tears in his eyes.

"Oh, my friend. This is a treat! I do not even know what all this will taste like."

"I'm pretty sure you're going to like it. Let's eat!" Collin announced, grinning. He was so pleased with Adelio's reaction. He decided he would have to bring different lunches every time now, just to see his friend's expression. He reached into the bags and pulled out cheeseburgers and fries, then set them in front of Adelio.

"After you, my friend. After you," Collin said, gesturing at the burger. Adelio picked up the burger, handling it awkwardly at first. Collin grabbed his own so he could demonstrate how to properly dig in to a burger. He didn't want Adelio to feel the least bit embarrassed. He took a deep breath then gave Adelio a thumbs up. "Go on. Take a bite."

He watched Adelio's expression as he took his first taste of

American food. At first Adelio frowned, concentrating on the new texture and taste. Then the frown melted into a soft expression of bliss. "Wonderful. Absolutely wonderful!" he said through a mouthful of burger.

Collin pulled out another cooler, this one filled with ice packs and cool drinks. He let Adelio choose from the variety of drinks then added one more surprise.

"For desert we have apple pie and plenty of it!"

When they'd finished the friends leaned back, rubbing their bellies and looking slightly sleepy.

"I do not know how to thank you for such a feast," Adelio said.

"There's no need. I'm just glad I could do it."

Adelio grinned. "I have a surprise for you as well, my friend," Adelio said, then released a low rumbling burp. He reached into the bag he'd brought and pulled out two cigars. "Cuban cigars. Now you are in for a real treat!"

Collin watched Adelio prepare the cigars with a cutter he'd pulled out of his pocket, then reach for matches.

"This is great," Collin said, grinning. "You're right. This is a real treat. It's illegal for Americans to buy Cuban cigars and bring them into the country. That's too bad because anyone can buy them and smoke them in other countries, like in Canada and England. I've heard they're terrific."

"Well," Adelio said, handing one cigar to Collin. "You're not buying a Cuban cigar or bringing it into your country, my friend. You are simply going to smoke a Cuban cigar."

Collin accepted the cigar. "Well, now that you put it that way I guess it's okay," he said, chuckling.

Adelio took another sip of his drink and set it down. "If your country would only lift the embargo, we could sell our cigars to America. Then maybe our country would not be so poor. I know they would want our cigars, and it seems to me that Americans spend a great deal of money on things they want. Maybe more than what they spend on things they need."

Collin laughed. "When my country lifts the embargo, your country will be overwhelmed by Americans." Adelio looked confused, and Collin clapped one friendly hand on his shoulder. "Cuba will be invaded by American tourists. As my mom always says, be careful what you wish for!"

Chapter 19

Cuban Departure Day 2

My shivering body welcomes the morning sun. I did not sleep well. It was cold during the night and my body needs to be warm. Especially with my sunburned skin. I should have brought a small blanket or sheet to use as a cover during the night, and to shield myself from the daytime sun. I never thought I would need a blanket. In my eagerness to leave I only thought about the necessities. I only brought the things I thought I absolutely needed. I should have let my wife help me with the details.

I should have brought a hat, too. My hands, face, neck, ears, feet and legs are severely burned. I tried to stay covered as much as I could during the day yesterday, but I did not do a very good job. I paddled for the majority of the day yesterday and when I did that I exposed most of my skin to the sun.

I need to paddle again today but I am not sure I will be able to do that. My muscles and hands are extremely sore, and I'm not sure the blisters on the palms of my hands can get any worse. I will do as much as I can.

It is very important that I paddle as much as possible because I do not want to get caught. I'm not sure how far away I am from either country now. If my calculations are correct, it should take me a minimum of two more full days to reach American waters. Late this evening will be the point when I have been out here for two full days. If I am spotted by a Cuban fishing boat or military plane before then, I will be caught. I must paddle harder today. I must.

I pray for good winds today. Winds that will help send me to America. If the wind pushes me towards Cuba I will only go backwards. No breeze is better than a bad wind.

I think it would be wise for me to rest a little while longer and let the sun warm my body. Then I will eat to keep up my strength. I can already tell the sun is going to be hot today. The morning air is heavy and the sky is clear with no clouds to give me any relief. This is going to be another long day.

I remember hearing of a newly married couple that left Cuba as I am doing. Their small vehicle was found abandoned near the beach. Nobody knows if they ever made it safely to America or whether they died during their journey. Their families claim they don't know anything about their illegal departure. Or if they do they aren't telling anyone. I wonder what provisions two people would have brought. I wonder if they brought a blanket.

I cannot imagine subjecting my wife and son to these elements. I would never have made them come, or have asked them to risk their lives. Especially my boy. If it was just my wife and I, perhaps she would be with me. But I could not bear seeing them suffer as I am now.

* * *

Evening

I paddled more today but not nearly as much as I wanted to. I was extremely tired. I paddled for a while then took a rest, then I tried to do more. My body is drained of strength. The palms of my hands are bleeding and I had to rip my shirt so I could wrap them. I should have done that to begin with so they would have been protected from the blisters. I never thought of that until yesterday.

I removed my long-sleeved shirt and submerged it in water, and the salt water stung my bleeding hands. I did not want to keep them in the water long because I know the sharks can smell blood from miles away. I used the wet shirt to cover my head and help keep me cool during the hottest hours of the day. Doing this exposed more of my upper body to the sun, but the drenched shirt did seem to help keep me cool.

It's cold again tonight. My shirt is not entirely dry because I kept it wet throughout the day, and now I can't stop shaking. I feel sick to my stomach. It would be a waste of food to try to eat. I most likely have sun poisoning. Nothing I can do about that now. To make it worse, the shivers will prevent me from getting any decent sleep.

I don't like night time on the water because I cannot see the creatures around me. A shark could easily attack my raft while I am asleep. Because of this I am hesitant to sleep for any long period of time. Not that I'll be able to sleep anyway, but I must stay aware of my surroundings. A few days without proper sleep will be worth it.

The authorities must be aware of my departure by now. They have more than likely questioned my wife, my family and friends. My wife and my son are the only people who know the truth of where I am and where I am going. They will not tell. My wife will pretend that I have left her and my son for another woman. She will cry the tears of a scorned woman and curse my existence to make them believe her story. The tears will come easy because she will be worried about me and miss me anyway. She cried when we rehearsed the possible questioning. It's what we planned and it was a good plan.

I miss my family. I don't even have a photo of them. I wish I could talk to them and hug them. I remind myself often that I am doing this because I love them. I cannot fail. Failing is not an option. I must succeed.

Only a few more days to go. I can do this.

Chapter 20

"What most people don't know," Collin said, "is that President Kennedy loved Cuban cigars. And before he signed the embargo he gave his press secretary less than twenty four hours to round up a bunch of his favorite Cuban cigars. The press secretary didn't let him down and he managed to scrounge up twelve hundred cigars for the President's personal stash." Collin chuckled, then continued, sounding subdued. "When you're the president of the United States, I suppose you can get just about anything you'd like."

Adelio dropped his chin to his chest and thought for a moment before speaking again. "My mother use to roll cigars when she was alive."

Collin held the cigar to his nose and inhaled its savory aroma. "I have been told that Cuban cigars are rolled on the thighs of young virgins," Collin said shyly. "Is that based on any kind of truth?"

The fact in question was one he'd heard from his father, and Collin was well aware that George could have been pulling his leg, as he so often did.

Adelio laughed. "Contrary to popular belief, no. They do not roll cigars on the thighs of virgins. That story, which became a legend, was made up many years ago. In the nineteenth century, actually. It was invented to encourage men to smoke more cigars, leading them to believe that they were smoking the essence of a virgin." Adelio shook his head, laughing at the gullibility of people. "And the crazy story worked! Our cigars are the most sought after in the world."

"And I, for one, am ready to smoke this one." Collin held the cigar between his thumb and forefinger, eager to try the world's most famous cigar. From everything he had heard, the Cuban cigar has no equal. He had been told it was like trying to compare California wine to French wine.

Adelio's expression was somber, as if he had something very important to impart. He held up a hand asking for patience.

"There are a few things you must know before smoking a Cuban cigar, my friend," Adelio said. "There continue to be known principless on this earth. If these principless are abused the most severe sort of subjective controversy may be created." He set the cigar between his lips and lit a small piece of cedar, holding the flame under the foot of the cigar without touching it. Then he gently drew the air in until the entire foot was alight and burning evenly.

Adelio slowly inhaled, then exhaled in the same manner. He held up one finger. "You should never drink beer from a coffee mug." A second finger joined the first. "You should never rob a bank without a gun and a dependable car." He took another draw from the cigar and closed his eyes as he breathed out. He put up a third finger. "And, my friend, it is important to always remember that a Cuban cigar is finer than your average smoke. It should be appreciated as the fine delicacy it is intended to be, for they are superior to any other cigar in this world."

Adelio smiled, satisfied, then handed Collin the box of matches. But he wasn't quite finished with his lesson yet.

"Smoking a Cuban cigar is an experience all to itself. You must smoke the cigar slowly, gently and meditatively. In this manner you will not miss the subtle flavor."

Collin did exactly as he'd been told and was glad of the lesson. Adelio was right. Taking the time to enjoy the cigar meant he appreciated it so much more.

"I have some other things for you, Adelio," Collin announced after a few moments of appreciative silence.

"Oh? And what is that?" Adelio asked. His voice sounded slow and relaxed, as if smoking the cigar put him in a meditative state.

Collin stood and lifted a panel under one of the seats. One by one he pulled out plastic shopping bags and handed them to Adelio, describing the contents as he went.

"Here we have soap," Collin announced, then grinned at Adelio's shocked expression. "Lots and lots of soap."

"And here we have several bags of sugar and salt. And ... let's see. Oh yes. This bag contains boxes of toothpaste and several toothbrushes." Adelio stared at the bags, stunned into speechlessness.

"Oh and in here we have tons of rice, beans and flour. I brought you different kinds of rice and beans, since I wasn't sure what you would like. I have to admit that I rarely went to the grocery store when I was younger. I found it too boring. My mom does all the shopping now. When I went this time I couldn't believe how many varieties of beans there are!"

Adelio looked for a moment as if he couldn't breathe. When he spoke his voice was filled with awe. "My friend, I can never thank you enough for your generosity. Never."

From that day forward Collin brought something new for Adelio to eat as well as a few bags of other items Collin had always taken for granted. He loved watching Adelio's reactions.

Adelio promised to bring some Cuban beer and rum for Collin to try, as well as some black bean soup. Collin declined the soup but was more than willing to try the alcohol.

The bond between Collin and Adelio grew stronger every year and they missed their visits when hurricane season hit. Whenever bad weather struck their meetings and business adventures were put on hold. But overall, they met quite often and both were always happy to share the latest news.

One day Adelio's boat came alongside Collin's, but Adelio wouldn't come aboard. Collin was suddenly wary, felt the hair rising on his arms. Adelio looked worried.

"Some men have been asking a lot of questions," Adelio said, his voice shaking.

"Who? What kind of questions?" Collin asked.

"I don't know for sure but it could be the human traffickers. They could be on to us," Adelio replied, sounding even more nervous. He glanced around him as if he feared he had been followed. "We don't want to get caught, my friend. I do not want to die. Not before I find my own freedom!"

"I completely agree with you," Collin said, trying to sound calm. But secretly, Collin's heart skipped with panic.

"We should take a break from transporting anyone for a while. We must stay under the radar and be safe."

Collin nodded. "I'm sure it's nothing. We'll be back in business again soon enough."

"I think we should stop our meetings as well, just in case they know something. It might be a while before I contact you." Adelio shifted from one foot to the other, clearly impatient to leave.

"Okay. I'll continue to check the online listings every morning. Get word to me if you find out something important," Collin shouted above the noise as Adelio started his boat engine.

Adelio started to pull away, then looked back at Collin and waved goodbye.

"We'll see each other soon!" Collin yelled. He raised his hand to wave farewell, thinking Adelio probably hadn't heard him over the sound of the engine. "Stay safe, my friend!"

Collin watched Adelio's boat skim across the water and felt suddenly sick to his stomach. He had to hope Adelio was just being overly paranoid, though he had rarely seen him behave that way. Still, it didn't hurt to take precautions, even if it was all over nothing. Collin nodded, trying to persuade himself that Adelio's fears were unfounded.

Their meeting had been very short, having lasted less than ten minutes. Adelio had clearly been shaken and upset, though he hadn't mentioned any specifics. Did he know something more than what he had told Collin? No. Collin couldn't believe that. Adelio was a friend. He would tell him if he knew anything more.

Collin stayed a while longer, staring at the sea and thinking hard. Home. I need to go home. He started his engine and turned his fishing boat about. He needed to get home and rest before Joey's graduation.

Chapter 21

Cuban Departure Day 3

The sun is trying to rise but it is having a hard time. Large clouds are keeping it at bay. A strong breeze is keeping me cool.

I am tired. My body aches, warning me not to move. My hands curl into claws because of the pain. The sun has blistered my burned skin, forming large, dark red blisters.

A storm is brewing. The wind is picking up and the water is getting choppy. The water jumping up and down makes it harder for me to locate shark fins. I hear thunder in the distance. It's the first real sound that I have heard in days.

If a bad storm is going to hit I would rather it be during the day than at night. It's bad enough being out here all alone and scared, but if the storm hits in the middle of the night and I have no light from the moon or the stars, everything would be even worse.

Before I set my raft into the water, I never thought about how lonely I would be out here. I suppose I never gave it a second thought. Not that it would have changed my decision to leave Cuba. I was too eager to leave. I was too eager to be free.

I can imagine my son leaving for school this morning after he hugs his mother. He will walk with his friends and laugh and talk the entire way. Some of his friends will ask him questions about me, but he will pretend he does not know. We practiced the questions before I left. It would have been easier on him if my wife and I had decided not to tell him anything, but I would not allow him to think that I abandoned him and his mother. I did not want him to think of me as a low sort of man.

My son is proud of me. He told me so. I know he misses me as I do him, but he also knows that I am doing this for his future.

My wife will work as much as she is allowed today. She will welcome our son home from school with hugs and kisses. I know she will cry a lot because I am gone. Our son is all she has left. She will think of me and no doubt imagine the worst. But when our son comes home, she will put on a happy face and smile for him.

They will keep each other company and talk about me during their evening meal. They will wonder if I made it to America. They will dream of me when they go to bed, just as I dream of them when I dare to close my eyes on this tiny raft.

I want a better life for them. They deserve a better life.

A few days of loneliness and pain will be worth it.

* * *

Evening

I thought I saw something like a raft in the distance today. Maybe it was someone else leaving Cuba. I listened for voices but heard nothing. I know I need medical help, but I kept quiet. Maybe I only saw a creature of the water. Maybe my fears are playing tricks on me. I would not doubt that. I am exhausted and starving and my body has been devastated by the sun and rain and cold.

There is no light tonight. The moon and stars are obscured behind the clouds that have hung over me all day. It's darker than dark can possibly be. The only light that I see is the lightning in the distance, and that is getting closer.

Heavy rain has been steady most of the day. I am freezing cold and shaking so much it's making my teeth chatter. I am soaked through. There is no point in my crying. If I cried the tears wouldn't be seen because of the rain streaming down my face. I am so dehydrated I might not be able to produce tears anyway.

The giant waves are like a most horrible ride. Up the wave and down the wave, making me sick. I grip the raft, trying to keep my balance, trying to hang on after the rainwater has made the raft slick. Some waves are taller than the tallest building I have ever seen. It's an amazing sight, but it's also scary. No boat will be on the water in this storm. There is no chance of a rescue tonight. I feel very small out on this water. I am unprotected and at the mercy of this fierce storm.

The longer I am out here, the more horror stories I recall of people whose journeys to America did not end well. I had always thought the stories could have been lies made up by the government to scare people so they wouldn't leave. I'm not sure anymore.

Over the noise of the storm I can barely hear myself weeping, though I can't tell if the water on my face is from tears or rain. I will cling to my miserable little raft this entire night, riding the ever-growing waves, praying it does not flip me. I am holding on for my life. I cannot let go.

The only things that keep my mind alive are the dreams I carry. I dream of the day when I am allowed to earn a decent living, when I am able to provide for my family in a respectable way. I dream of buying more food than what is allocated to us so that we will not worry about our next meal. We will eat eggs and bacon for breakfast every morning. We will eat meat every day. And we will have fresh bread with every meal.

We will buy a home which the government will not own. We will buy as many seeds as we want and have our own garden. My wife has always wanted a garden, but we could never get permission to buy seeds. It is sad because in Cuba only farmers that are overseen by the government can buy seeds to grow vegetables. And they are only allowed to grow so much. The lands have gone to waste.

Tomorrow is day number four. If my calculations are correct I should find land or at least be found by Americans tomorrow. If only I can live that long.

Chapter 22

May 2011

One year. It was hard to believe it had been one year since George and Betty had died.

It had also been just over a year since he had heard from Adelio. He had heard nothing from his friend. Adelio had not even contacted him through an online listing, which had been their normal routine.

Collin finished unpacking the boxes and put the contents in appropriate places around on the yacht.

One year. So much could happen in one year.

When his parents had been killed, he had not been able to confide in his friend. Surely Adelio would have had some comforting words for Collin since he had lost both of his parents as well. That would have been worse in a way, he admitted, because Adelio's parents had died when he was younger. He'd had to provide for himself from a very young age.

For the thousandth time, Collin checked the online listings. Nothing. He felt helpless and frustrated. All he could do was hope

Adelio was okay. He had seemed so frightened the last time they'd met.

Adelio could have been right when they had met the last time, but Collin didn't want to even consider that possibility. He had to assume Adelio was okay, just playing it safe. Sure. That's all it was. Playing it safe.

But for an entire year?

After Collin had finished unpacking the boxes he decided to clean up some of the mess on his fishing boat, make it a bit more presentable. Then he might take it out for a while. It had also been a year since he had taken his fishing boat anywhere, and though he had been consumed by grief and distracted by alcohol, Collin had missed being on the water. It was time to get back out.

Joey was at the library. Knowing him, he would be there all day and probably most of the evening. If Collin left now he would be back before Joey even got home. Not that it mattered. Even if Collin got home after Joey was already in, Joey wouldn't mind. He would be glad that his useless big brother had at least done something. Anything was better than doing nothing.

Collin pushed off from the dock, comforted by the familiar sound of his boat's engine. He didn't know where he was going; it was just important that he go. As he got into the open water he opened up the throttle, needing to feel the wind whip against his face and through his hair. The tang of salty air in his nose and the sounds of the birds and splashing water felt genuinely good. He took a long, deep breath, enjoying the day. It felt therapeutic to be back on the water again.

Time flew by, and by the time he looked at his watch it was already five o'clock. Without even realizing what he had done, Collin found himself pulling up at one of the places where he and Adelio had so often met at in the past.

From a distance, Collin noticed another fishing boat speeding toward him. He felt a pang of nerves ripple through him at the unexpected sight. Who was this? He pulled out his binoculars from under a bench and studied the approaching boat. Amazingly, it looked like Adelio's fishing boat. Collin frowned, scratching his head as the boat drew nearer.

Then he lowered the binoculars, mouth hanging open with amazement. The other boat contained none other than Adelio.

"What the hell?" Collin mumbled. He felt an odd mixture of elation and fury at the sight of his old friend. Had Adelio been coming out here all this time without him? What was going on? But at the sight of his friend's open grin, he dropped his anger.

"Adelio! Where have you been, man?" Collin cried, waving in

excitement as the boat came alongside. "I haven't heard from you in a year!"

"Hello, my friend!" Adelio called, smiling as he waved back. "How have you been? Good, I hope."

A thousand emotions swirled through Collin's heart as he tied his friend's boat to his. "No, Adelio, I cannot say I am good. A lot has happened. But I'm so relieved to see you. I was so afraid something horrible had happened to you."

Adelio embraced him as usual and the two men held on just a moment longer, enjoying each other's presence once again. Then Collin pulled away and frowned down at the shorter man.

"Why haven't you contacted me? I checked online every day for a year and you've left nothing, not even one word. What was I supposed to think?"

"I'm sorry, Collin. Truly, I am. It hasn't been very safe this past year. I would have contacted you, but I didn't want to put you in any danger," Adelio replied. Then he frowned back at Collin. "Are you all right, my friend? You look as if you've been ill. You have lost a lot of weight since the last time I saw you."

Collin shrugged, trying to contain his emotions. He didn't want to burst into tears in front of Adelio, but the urge was there. "No, actually, I'm not really all right. A lot has happened, like I said. Just after the last time I saw you, my parents were killed." Collin looked away. "I could have used a friend."

"I'm so sorry, my friend," Adelio said gently. "I didn't know. If I had known ... I'm sorry. I am very sorry."

"How could you know?" Collin kept his eyes averted. He wanted to clear his thoughts, move on, but he was too torn up. He wasn't angry with Adelio. No, it was worse than that. He was disappointed and felt he had been let down. Not only had Collin lost his parents, but he also felt as if he'd lost his friend.

"Again, I'm sorry," Adelio said. "I wish I could have been here for you. I know what it feels like to lose your parents, but not at the same time. I am sorry."

Collin sighed. "I'm sorry too, Adelio. I don't mean to take this out on you. It's just that I needed a friend. That's all. Anyway, today I'm just happy as hell to see you again. Enough about me. How are your wife and baby? Did you have a boy or a girl?"

Now it was Adelio's turn to look away, but Collin could see sadness fill his dark eyes. Collin felt immediately guilty. Something was very wrong, but he'd been so consumed by his own selfish rant he hadn't spared a thought for his friend.

"My wife and baby died during child birth. She got sick a few days before going into labor. After that she was too weak. The baby was stillborn." He sniffed and wiped a hand over his eyes. "It was a boy," he said softly.

Collin set his hand on Adelio's shoulder and squeezed gently. "I'm the one who should be sorry, Adelio. I didn't know of your loss either, and you needed a friend too. I'm sorry I wasn't here for you. I'm very sorry for your loss."

Collin didn't know what else to say. He and Joey had heard those same words over and over at his parents' funeral, but he'd never had to say it to anyone before. "I'm sorry for your loss," had always seemed like something people said when they didn't really know what else to say. At the time, he'd gotten so tired of hearing those words. It surprised him to hear his own voice saying the same ones to Adelio.

Chapter 23

Collin abruptly changed the subject. He didn't want to speak about death anymore. It was too painful. "Have you been out here much in the past year?"

"Yes. I have been coming two to three days a week, hoping to catch you out on the water," Adelio said. "I've been wondering what happened to you as well. I assumed that I would see you, but you never came. I thought something bad might have happened to you." Adelio lowered his eyes. "And it had."

Collin shook his head. "But I've been checking online every day, and I didn't see anything from you. I would never have thought you'd be here. Today was a total coincidence," Collin blurted. "Up until today, I hadn't been on the water for an entire year."

"I couldn't risk contacting you online. So I continued to come here," Adelio replied. "But how could you have known? Our last meeting was so short, and I'm sorry for that".

"I never would have thought to come out here. You seemed so concerned that I figured this was the last place you'd come. Anyway," he said, grinning, "I'm just glad you're okay. I've been worried about you."

"I've been worried about you, too," Adelio replied, smiling back at Collin. "Shall we do some fishing?"

Collin and Adelio fished and talked for hours, going well into the evening. For Collin this evening's chance meeting changed everything. A small piece of his life, which he'd thought had been lost, had returned. He had his friend back, someone to talk to. He knew he'd always had Joey, but it just wasn't the same as having a best friend in whom he could confide. From this point on he felt confident life would get better.

By the end of the evening Collin had gained an optimistic new outlook on life. He felt encouraged and strong enough to once again take control of his life. It was time to get back to work and take care of Joey, and make sure he went to college. It was time to "grow up", as Joey would say.

Adelio tucked his fishing gear away in his boat and asked Collin if he'd like to meet up again in a few days.

"That'd be great," Collin said, already looking forward to seeing his friend again. This is what he needed. Just to be able to talk to someone and lift his spirits. Collin felt like a weight had been lifted off his shoulders. In the last moment, though, his mind flashed over what Adelio was now going home to. No wife, no baby, no food, no hope.

"Adelio," Collin said quietly.

Adelio looked up, concerned when he heard Collin's serious tone. "Yes?"

"Come with me. Get in my boat and just come with me. Come to America. It's your turn, man. It's time for you to find your own freedom and have a new life."

Adelio grinned. "I will think about it."

"What is there to think about? I'm sorry to be so blunt, but from what you have told me, you have nothing left in Cuba. Why not just come with me now? What is there to think about? You could live with me and Joey for as long as you want."

Collin got more animated as he spoke, realizing it was an actual possibility now. "You could have a new life. A wonderful life! No more rations, no more worrying about where you're going to get your next meal. Come with me, Adelio. Just do it. Get on my boat right now and come with me to America."

From the way Adelio bit his lip, from the way he blinked a little more quickly, Collin could see his friend was seriously considering the offer. He hoped with all his heart that he would accept.

But Adelio slowly shook his head, and twisted his mouth in an apologetic smile. "What about the other people? Those that still want to go to America? What about them? Who will take them?

What I do … What we do … makes a difference to so many people." Adelio placed a hand on Collin's shoulder and nodded seriously. "I promise that I will think about it and give you an answer soon."

As Adelio's boat began moving away he yelled back over his shoulder at Collin. "I haven't had an Italian Beef in a year!"

"Allow me to do the honors," Collin called back. "See you in a few days."

"I'll bring the cigars and beer," Adelio said, waving as he pulled away. "See you then!"

Collin watched the other boat leave and was filled with hope at the possibility that in just a few short days Adelio might be boarding his boat with his bags packed, ready to move to America. He was looking forward to finally introducing Adelio to Joey and their friends.

A humming drone from a distance jerked Collin's thoughts back to reality and he stared out at the sea. From beyond Adelio's boat he could see lights. It looked like two separate boats. One of them was heading towards Adelio's boat, and it looked as if it were practically flying across the water. The other boat seemed to get faster by the second, and it was headed directly toward Collin.

Panicked thoughts raced through Collin's mind. Who was in the boat? Was it the Coast Guard? Had they been caught? No! The

Coast Guard couldn't be coming for them, because they had done nothing wrong. There were no Cubans on board. They hadn't even transported anyone for a year. Stay calm, he told himself. Everything will be fine.

But the approaching boat wasn't slowing. He could see the profiles of men standing on deck and he squinted hard, searching for uniforms.

"Just stay calm," he told himself over and over again.

It was not the U.S. Coast Guard. The boat had Cuban colors: black, red and white. And the men standing on deck didn't look like anyone in authority, either. Collin's stomach lurched. That meant it had to be the traffickers. The worst possibility was about to come true and there wasn't a damn thing he could do about it.

Collin straightened, feeling a brief flash of hope. He was on the American side of the Florida Strait. That must mean he was safe. But no. Whoever was in the rapidly approaching boat either did not know, or did not care. His stomach rolled up his throat and he tasted bile.

If Collin hadn't been daydreaming about his day, and if it hadn't been so dark, he might have had enough time to notice the Cuban boat, start his engine and put some distance between them. Then he could have contacted the U.S. Coast Guard for assistance. But it was too late now. The boat had already come alongside. For the first time since his parents' death, Collin was scared. He didn't know what to do.

The men in the boat glared at Collin, but he didn't say a word. What could he say? What were they going to do to him? He started to tremble, feeling deep vibrations run up and down his spine like an engine. He didn't want the men to see he was afraid, so he clenched his fists to his sides until his knuckles turned white.

It happened so fast. In an instant three Cuban men had leapt into Collin's boat, and before he could say a word two of the men had grabbed his arms. A third man looked Collin straight in the eyes, drew back his right arm and balled his hand into a fist. Collin suddenly snapped out of his stupor and realized what was going to happen. His eyes widened and he struggled, trying to loosen the other men's holds on him.

"Wait!" Collin yelled. But the fist crashed into Collin's face before he could say another word.

Confusion … stars … darkness.

Chapter 24

Cuban Departure Day 4

I am alive. My body aches all over as if it is completely broken. I know I must have fallen asleep sometime during the night because my eyes were crusted shut with salt water when I woke.

The sun is rising. My blistered skin stings with every breath I take. My eyes are swollen and dry and feel as if they have been sprinkled with hot sand. My lips are cracked and bleeding, tasting like metal. I feel the warmth of the sun but my body continues to shake. I am dehydrated and starving. I am in urgent need of medical attention.

My raft is barely holding together. It feels as if it will fall apart at any moment. Again I will spend my day grasping to the raft, terrified that it will leave me. I must hold it together. I need to stay out of the water and away from the hungry jaws of sharks.

I lost most of my supplies during the storm. My knife and compass I could have gone without, but my entire food sack and most of my water supply was stolen by the storm, as if it had been a thief in the night.

I still have a small amount of food left in my pocket, but not enough. And a few ounces of water, maybe enough for a baby to sip on. I would have traded all of my food to keep my water.

I will be forever grateful that my wife and son did not come with me on this journey. We would not have had enough food or water. The raft is barely keeping me afloat. It would not have been able to hold us all.

One day I plan to tell my son the story of the raging storm. I will tell him that I was scared, but he won't believe me. I am his father and I am not supposed to be afraid of anything. He will enjoy such a tale.

Today should be my last day on this forsaken water. I will find land or I will be found. I have no options. I will either find my freedom or I will die on this water.

Today is the day. I can do this.

* * *

Evening

I did not find land today. I was not found either. I believe the waves and winds of the storm have blown my raft off course.

Where am I? Am I closer to America? Or am I somewhere in the middle of nowhere? I am lost.

If I had not left Cuba I would be with my family. I would have at least eaten a small meal this evening and I would be safe. I would not be thirsty. I would not be burned or in pain. Did I make the right decision, leaving them for a dream?

The water is finally calm. Before the sun went down I saw sharks in the distance, slowly circling my raft. They know I am here. Are they close? I cannot see them for the darkness. I can hear splashes on the silent water where before I heard nothing. The sharks are waiting for me. Watching me. They are always hungry. I must stay quiet. I must stay awake.

I begin to cry again. I've cried more during this journey than I have throughout my entire life. I need comfort but nobody is with me to ease my pain. Can my wife feel my pain? Does she hear my cries?

I am not certain how many more days I will live without food or water. I don't believe I can do this any longer.

Chapter 25

What's that damn sound? The noise was something sudden, something fierce. The sound of rain pelting down on metal came to mind.

Collin struggled through the murk of confusion, reaching towards consciousness. When at last he was lucid, he realized he lay on hard dirt, his back in agony, hands fumbling towards his aching head.

"He's finally waking up. Hey, asshole. Are you going to get up today?" The strange voice was deep and heavily accented. He kicked Collin hard in the foot.

"What day is it?" Collin asked. How long had he been here, wherever that was? He pressed his hands over his eyes and smelled dry dirt.

"What day is it?" The man repeated, his tone mocking. "Well, today is your lucky day! You know why? Because you're still alive." The man hooted with laughter. "Your lucky day. That's what day it is!" He shuffled away, dragging his feet and stirring up dust. "He's waking up, Neo! See to it he gets something to eat and drink."

A metal door slammed shut and Collin opened his eyes, trying to identify where he was. He stared up at the ceiling of some type of warehouse he'd never seen before, or at least he didn't think he had. From where he lay he could hear the ocean, the rain, the sound of boats, and people outside. He must be on a dock at a port somewhere. But where? And how did he get here?

The metal door scraped open and a pair of feet thumped quickly along the dirt floor.

"You're awake I see. This is good. Here's some water and biscuits. My name is Neo. They will be coming for you soon, my friend. So listen carefully. I must go."

Neo knelt next to Collin and whispered close to his face. "They brought you in late last evening. I heard them saying that you, a dirty American, had been stealing from them, taking their workers to America, and that they are losing money because of you and your friend." Neo spoke so fast that Collin could barely keep up.

"Your friend is there," Neo said and pointed towards the other end of the warehouse. When Collin squinted he could see the still body of a man, curled on his side. "I must go now, but if you value your life you must listen to me now. Do whatever they say. Find your way back home. I cannot help anymore. God be with you and keep you safe."

Neo quickly turned to leave. As he opened the door, Collin could see that he'd been right: he was on a dock, surrounded by boats. Men loitered outside the door, drinking and laughing as if nothing were wrong. The warehouse was small, shabby and poorly built. Any windows had been painted over in order to obscure any proper light from entering the room, as well as to prevent anyone from either looking out or looking in. The tin roof was thin and the sound of every rain drop echoed throughout the building.

Collin managed to get to his feet, trying not to make a sound. He didn't want to attract any attention. Moving slowly, he made his way to the other end of the warehouse, heading towards the prone body of the man in the corner.

With a groan, Collin leaned down and saw that it was indeed Adelio, lying on his side in the dirt. Someone had beaten Adelio badly. His face was bruised and swollen. Open cuts and streaks of dried blood almost completely covered his face and neck. There was blood on his torn shirt as well. His hands were bruised and swollen, as if he had fought back.

Collin shook Adelio gently. "Adelio! Adelio!" he whispered urgently. "Can you hear me? Come on man, wake up! It's me, Collin!"

Adelio groaned as he slowly regained consciousness. "Collin?" he croaked, his voice scratchy. He looked genuinely shocked. "What are you doing here?

"Adelio! What is going on? Where are we? What happened to you?" Collin heard himself peppering Adelio with questions, just like his brother always did to him. He didn't pause for answers but demanded them just the same. "Who did this to you?"

"We are in Cuba in a small fishing village. You must go! You must leave! They will kill us both!" Adelio blurted.

Collin watched him reach for a small bucket of water by his head and struggle with it, eventually taking a gulp. He choked down the water then quickly took a few more large mouthfuls before he choked and began spewing water with every cough. After a few minutes he settled down, but kept a tight grip on the bucket. His eyes were deep with remorse when he looked up at Collin.

"Who are they?" Collin demanded. "And don't tell me to leave. I'm not gonna just leave you here. You know that. What's going on? Why are we here?"

"Collin, my friend, they are the traffickers. They are angry with us for transporting Cuban citizens to America. Somehow we were found out. Someone must have betrayed me." Adelio struggled to sit up and Collin helped him by placing a strong hand under his elbow.

A look of despair came across Adelio's face "They've known for a very long time. Collin, I have something terrible to tell you, and I know you will hate me for all time when you learn this. I overheard them talking earlier. These men, they are responsible for the deaths of your parents. The explosion was never meant for them. They meant to kill you."

The floor suddenly felt wobbly and Collin slammed his hands flat to hold himself upright. This was all a bad dream. It had to be. But no. This made sense. Betty and George had died when they started his car. It should have been him, not them.

Collin rested his head in the palms of his hands as tears rushed to his eyes. For the past year he had felt accountable for the deaths of his parents because of the faulty gas line in his car. Now he knew that he was entirely to blame. If he had not been transporting Cubans to America these men would not have killed his parents. There was no faulty fuel line, only faulty thinking on his part. He would always have that burden to bear.

"There is one more thing, my friend. It's your brother," Adelio said.

Collin dropped his hands and stared straight into Adelio's eyes.

"What about my brother?" Collin demanded.

"Joey. He is here. They have him."

"What? Joey?! They have Joey?!" Collin cried, then started sobbing. "Oh my God. What have I done? What have I done?" Collin brought his fisted hands to the sides of his head. His parents were dead because of him, and now they had his brother.

"Where is he?"

"I don't know. I just heard them talking. You must find your brother quickly, Collin. You must leave this place and go home. Find a way! Find a new life so they cannot find you again. Our business together is over, you must understand. We must go our separate ways and you must go now. Take your brother and go!" Adelio said firmly.

Collin's heart thundered; the dust on his hands had turned to mud with sweat. "Where is Joey? Where exactly are we?"

"We are in Cuba. You know your way home. Only ninety miles through the Strait. But you must find your brother. Take a boat and just go." Adelio said, then choked down more water to ease his tortured throat. His eyes darted beyond Collin and reflected sudden panic. "They are coming!"

Adelio struggled with a necklace he wore, tugging it out from within his shirt. A cross dangled from the old string. Collin helped his friend when he had trouble, then was surprised when Adelio thrust it towards him.

"I want you to have this," Adelio whispered. "My father gave it to me before he left on his journey. I want you to take it and keep it safe. Now go, Collin. May God be with you. I am a dead man."

Chapter 26

Without pausing to think, Collin slipped the necklace over his head. He needed his hands free so he could help his friend. "I can't just leave you here! Come on, Adelio. We can find Joey and leave together. You can finally come to America!"

But Adelio's eyes, dark within the mass of cuts and bruises covering his face, suddenly pooled with fear. The hand Collin held between his own started to shake. Collin heard the voices of several men coming closer to the warehouse door. The door slammed open and two men stepped inside, letting it close with a thud behind them. Their stride suggested they owned the place, and Collin wasn't about to argue. Both men were of average height and were stocky. Neither one of their expressions was forgiving in the least.

To his surprise, they ignored Adelio and stood by Collin instead. One of the men clucked his tongue with mock sympathy. "Collin, Collin," he said with a deep sigh. "Oh, how you disappoint us. Did you think we would never find out? Did you think we would never find you? Do you not know who you are dealing with?"

Collin stared, mute with terror.

The man chuckled and tucked his thumbs into the waistband of his jeans. He leaned against a wooden post and smiled down at Collin. "Please excuse my manners. Let me introduce myself. My name is Pello, and this is my friend, Arlo. Hey, Arlo. Say hello to our new friend." Arlo nodded towards Collin, not saying a word. He was a big man, with broad, muscular shoulders.

Pello spoke very good English and his clothes were those of a well-dressed punk. He wore a button-down white silk shirt under a black leather jacket, though the warehouse was warm. His jeans and boots looked expensive. The dim light of the warehouse reflected off a flashy gold watch and a number of rings on his fingers. His hair was slicked back and he wore a thick gold chain. Whether he had money or not, he wanted people to think he did. The half-smoked cigar between his fingers needed to be lit.

"We do not like to be played with, Collin. That is the rule of the game," Pello said, his cheerful voice turning grievous. "We do not like having things stolen from us. And most of all, we do not like losing money."

Pello suddenly grabbed Collin by the hair and yanked his head back, then leaned in close so that he was within inches of Collin's face. "You owe us!" he screamed, spit gathering at the corners of his mouth. "And you will pay! You will never do this again!" Pello's fist tightened on Collin's hair then thrust him to the side with all his strength, smashing Collin's face into the ground. When Collin tried to lift his head he could taste blood running down his lips.

Pello stood up straight, keeping his eyes on Collin, then snapped at his partner. "Arlo. Bring him to me!"

Arlo nodded once then turned and strode to the door. He stepped outside, leaving the door open behind him, and Collin felt a breath of rain-soaked breeze trickle through the warehouse. Arlo's voice was muffled, but Collin could hear him speaking to a few men who were grunting something back.

All the time he was gone, Pello stood silently over Collin, his arms folded across his chest.

Then Arlo appeared in the doorway again. He traipsed slowly but purposefully toward Collin, his large hand locked tightly on the back of Joey's neck. Joey's hands were tied in front and he was stumbling, struggling to walk straight. His eyes were wide, and he kept trying to turn his head to talk to Arlo, who ignored him.

"What's going on?" Joey cried. Collin's heart broke, hearing the bewilderment in his little brother's voice. "Who are you? Where are you taking me? I haven't done anything wrong. You have the wrong person!"

As Arlo and Joey came closer, Collin could see that Joey had been beaten as well. His lip was swollen and his nose was obviously broken. Tears mixed with fresh blood as it slowly streamed down the side of his face from a cut just above his eyebrow. Joey was badly hurt. How much torture had they put him through? How much could an innocent nineteen year old boy endure?

Collin fought to keep the rage out of his eyes. He wanted to pound Pello, beat him to a bloody pulp. Killing him would be even better. But he had to stay calm if he were going to get the three of them out alive.

These men could have guns. Probably did. In reality, they could easily have killed both Joey and Adelio by now, but they hadn't. Maybe this was just a warning. Maybe they only wanted to scare them and would let them leave. That would be just fine with Collin. He would accept the warning and would never, ever do anything like this again. No more transporting. Lesson learned. All he wanted was to go home and forget about all of this.

Arlo gave Joey a hard shove towards Collin, taking Joey off guard so that he stumbled and rolled onto the ground. Joey tried to sit up, then collapsed again, looking up at Collin with liquid eyes. He didn't say a word, but Collin saw both terror and relief in those familiar eyes. Joey was comforted to see Collin there. Collin would save him, take him away from this nightmare.

"Collin!" Pello shouted, black eyes like onyx. "You have taken from us, and you must be punished. It's time for you to learn your lesson. Arlo, if you please!"

Joey looked at Collin, confused, but Collin said nothing. Arlo nodded coolly at Pello then reached behind his back and withdrew a small pistol. He aimed the barrel straight at Adelio, who struggled desperately to get to his feet. Arlo pulled the trigger and Adelio fell to the ground, a bullet in his head. Adelio was dead.

"NO!" Collin cried over Joey's petrified screams. He reached for Adelio, his entire body on fire with shock. This couldn't be happening. This was all too real. When he glanced at Joey, his little brother was staring at him, face slick with tears and blood.

Pello took the gun from Arlo, then pointed it at Collin. "So, my friend, as I said before, it is time for you to learn your lesson." Pello's aim immediately shifted towards Joey, and the gun went off. Joey grunted and curled instantly into a ball, grabbing desperately for Collin's arm. Pello had shot him in the stomach.

Collin grabbed Joey and screamed at Pello, his breath coming in quick sobs. "Stop this! Stop this now! I haven't transported anyone in a year! I quit a long time ago! Why? Why would you do this? Joey didn't do anything to you!"

Joey hadn't done anything wrong. Neither had Betty or George, but all of this was entirely Collin's fault. Adelio lay dead beside him and somehow Collin was to blame for that as well.

Joey was all that he has left in this world, and he was bleeding heavily from his stomach, a dark puddle pooling in the dirt. Collin shook his head hard. Joey couldn't die. He wouldn't let him go.

Pello's smile was calm and serene. As if he were doing nothing more than disciplining a stubborn child. "As I said before, you must learn your lesson. Your friend is dead, and your brother will not live long. This will be a very painful death, I'm afraid. You will stay here and watch your brother die, then I will come back to teach you your final lesson."

Pello and Arlo turned and left the building. Collin held Joey as tightly as he could, and Joey whimpered in pain.

"God it hurts," Joey said through clenched teeth. His hand pressed hard over his stomach. "Am I going to die?"

Collin shook his head fiercely. "Not if I can help it, you're not. Don't even think that way, you hear me? Say it again and I'll kick your ass!" Collin growled. He looked around the warehouse, seeking some kind of answer, then laid his brother gently onto the ground. "We need to get out of here. I need to get you to a doctor." Fumbling as quickly as he could with his trembling fingers, Collin took off his button-down shirt, then yanked off his white tank and placed it on Joey's stomach. "Here, hold this on the wound. Keep pressure on it."

Collin got to his feet and studied the painted windows. Could they simply crawl out through one of them? Could it be that easy? But moving Joey would be difficult. Maybe Pello had felt safe leaving them alone because he'd known Collin would never leave Joey, and Joey was too badly off to go anywhere.

"Come on Joey, we're getting out of here," Collin said, hoisting Joey to his feet. Joey groaned, doubled over in pain. He struggled to cling to Collin's arm. "We have to go through the window, Joey. Do you think you can do it?"

"No," Joey said weakly. "I don't think I can."

But he had no choice. If they didn't do something, they would both be dead very soon. "Well, suck it up. Sorry, but you're going through the window. You can cry all you want but you'll have to do that later. Right now we have to go home," Collin said, then grinned briefly at Joey. "You know, I've often wanted to put you through a window. Now I finally get my chance."

Joey gasped. "Stop," he begged. "It hurts when I laugh."

Chapter 27

Cuban Departure Day 5

The sun will rise whether I live or die. It does not care about me. It is going to be hot again today, but I have nothing left to sweat.

The sharks did not attack me. If they had tried I would not have been able to fight them.

I barely slept, only listened to the splashing of the water. I know the sharks were close, and I know there were many around me, but they did not attack. It was a good thing the moon did not light the water during the night because I did not want to see their fins. I kept very quiet.

I can barely move. I am too weak. My blistered, rashed skin tears itself open, then bleeds. My eyes are nearly swollen shut and I can taste blood in my mouth from my cracked lips. What is keeping me alive? Why am I still here?

I have no food or water. What I do have are many regrets. Maybe I should never have left Cuba. I should have planned better and built a sturdier raft, more secure. I should have made sure I had shelter and brought more food.

The sea is endless around me, but I cannot drink the water that I float upon. This water takes me to freedom, but I cannot drink it or death will come to me even sooner. I do not want to die, but sometimes I wonder if it might be a relief.

The only thing I can do is dream of my family. That also hurts. I am too weak to cry. I just lie here, doing nothing.

* * *

Evening

Awareness comes and goes. I have been in and out of consciousness all day. My brain, which barely thinks anymore, tells me this is most likely a result of the combination of heat and being deprived of food and water.

I doubt I will make it through another night. I can barely hold onto the raft. If the sharks find me tonight, they will eat me. If another storm comes it will kill me. If I move my raft will fall apart. I do not move.

My family will wonder if I have already made it to America. My wife will be counting the days until I contact her. My son will be dreaming of a new life in America, one where he will eat and live in a strange new world of freedom.

If I die they will not hear from me, and they will think I deserted them. Or they will correctly fear the worst. Do they worry for me? Yes. I know they do. I am glad they do not know what I have been going through. I am glad they cannot see me. It would make them sad.

Will I find freedom or death? At this point, I would welcome either one. Whichever it is, I hope it comes swiftly.

I think it will be death. I am done counting the days. I do not have the strength left in me to fight for my freedom. My dream of America is slipping away. I only wanted a good life for my family. Was I asking too much? Was I wrong for wanting a better life for them? I thought I was doing the right thing.

I see now that I was being selfish.

My son will grow up without a father. He will not have me around to teach him to be a man. He will forget me. He will eventually marry and have his own family. I will never see my son or my grandchildren.

My wife and I will not grow old together as we always promised each other. I will never again hold her in my arms and tell her that I love her. She will not be allowed to marry again because they will not be able to find my body. She will be alone with the exception of my son. She will be sad and she will cry many tears. I hope she will forgive me.

The cool air is making me shiver again. Splashes in the water are getting closer, telling me the sharks are near. They have been following me and waiting for the perfect time to attack. They prey on the weak.

They nudge at my raft now, trying to find its weakness. It won't take them long. It is barely holding together and it will be easy for their sharp teeth to tear it apart. They are right here, closer than I even imagined. If I wanted, I could reach out and touch them.

They will not relent tonight. They will take what they have come for, and that is me.

This will be a horrible way to die.

I never thought I would give up hope, but nothing can save me now. Dreams of a better life in America will never come true. It was all for nothing.

I cannot do this anymore.

Chapter 28

The small window stuck, jammed by years of disuse and peeling paint. Collin took a deep breath and leaned against it, jarring loose the adhesion. He grunted quietly with effort until he was able to finally open it, forcing it into as large a hole as possible. Warm wet air rushed in, bringing with it a terrible odor of rot. Rain continued to pour down, which was good. Its noise would keep the sounds of their escape to a minimum. The hot, stinky air and rain mixing together would create a low, thick fog that would help to hide them. There was very little light. What there was of it appeared to come from the front of the buildings and warehouses, beaming from well-spaced lamps and dissolving into the fog.

Collin quickly identified the source of the smell. Behind the warehouse sat a few dumpsters, overflowing with trash. The stench was overwhelming, enough to make Collin gag. Something moved, catching his eye, then another small movement to the side. Collin shuddered involuntarily. Rats. And from the look of it, a lot of rats. He looked more closely at the garbage and was able to make out the shapes of the vermin, swarming through the piles.

With tremendous effort and maneuvering, Collin was able to

help Joey through the window, constantly worried that Pello and Arlo would return and discover them. Joey gritted his teeth against the pain, taking deep gulps of air that he held for thirty seconds then slowly released.

Behind the warehouse Collin could make out the profiles of other rundown buildings and warehouses built extremely close to each other. If Collin and Joey could stay hidden behind the buildings, they could have a chance of getting away. The few dingy lamp posts leaned as if they could fall at any moment, their light was very dim.

Collin gently wrapped his arm around Joey's waist, half-carrying him behind the buildings. At the end of each building he hesitated, leaned Joey against the wall and peered around the corner. He wasn't sure yet of their destination, and for the moment he was focused more on staying out of sight.

Joey's consciousness dwindled and Collin had to keep him both calm and alert. "Joey, how did you end up here?" Collin asked, trying to keep Joey distracted from the pain.

Joey gasped in a breath before speaking. "My friends brought me. Or at least I thought they were my friends."

"What friends?" asked Collin.

"You know. The guys that would stop by once in a while, hanging out in front of the house. They drove a blue car, remember?

Sometimes when I checked the mail they would just happen to be driving by and they'd stop and talk for a bit. They invited me to go boating with them," Joey muttered wryly. "Sure sounded like fun at the time."

Collin remembered the sweet blue car, could picture it clearly in his mind. He'd seen it that morning after Joey had chewed him out for always being drunk. It was the morning of the first anniversary of their parents' death. Joey had stormed out the front door to check the mail and Collin had, through the window, seen Joey meet up with the men in the car. Collin felt ill at the thought. They had befriended Joey in order to get to Collin, because they were working for the traffickers.

Joey's voice was weak but he kept on talking. Maybe he knew it was good to be distracted. Collin didn't care why. He was just happy to encourage Joey. Though the whole story only made Collin feel worse, he needed to know.

"They told me," Joey suddenly sucked in air through his teeth and flinched. A sting of pain held him hostage for a couple of breaths. When he looked back at Collin his eyes looked flat, as if he fought back not only the pain, but the thoughts behind them. "They said they had recently moved to Key West and were new to the area. They told me they lived in the neighborhood. I went on a few boat rides with them, did some fishing, no big deal, really. They seemed nice enough."

Joey paused for a moment and his whole face seemed to harden before Collin's eyes. "Pello, he told me what you did, or what you use to do," Joey said. "He told me you brought illegal Cubans to America." Collin said nothing, only waited, so Joey went on, sounding cooler than ever.

"Pello also said that he hadn't meant to kill Mom and Dad. That he hadn't meant to kill them, Collin! That he had meant to kill you instead. Pello killed our parents, Collin. It wasn't an accident!"

Collin swallowed hard. It must have been overwhelming for Joey to hear all this. It had been hard enough for Collin, and he'd at least had some idea of what was going on.

"So the guys came by and invited me to go fishing with them that day, and I went. We were farther out in the ocean than normal and when I asked about where we were going to fish, they started laughing. They told me that someone wanted to talk to me about you. One thing lead to another and they ganged up and beat the shit out of me. The next thing I knew, I woke up here, in Cuba no less. Collin, what's going on?"

"Let's go," Collin said, helping him run again.

When they had gone past about twenty buildings, Collin looked around one wall and recognized a man he'd met only briefly: Neo, the Cuban who had given him food when he'd first woken up.

"My friend! You're alive!" Neo exclaimed in a whisper, then looked furtively around. "You must leave! You must go before they know you're gone."

"Can you help us? We need a boat," Collin asked.

"Yes! Yes! Come. Follow me, but be quick!" Neo said. With a wave of his hand he signaled for Collin and Joey to follow him toward the docks.

"You see? Look there!" Neo said. He pointed down the dock, three boats away. It was Adelio's boat.

"Here. Take my jacket and hat!" Neo said firmly, putting them on Joey. "When you walk down the docks do not act as if you are in pain, amigo. Your life depends upon this. Walk straight and tall and normally, not slow. Do not slouch. You must act normal or you will get caught again. The men, they are busy. They like to drink too much and be with women, you see. I will follow a little behind you, to try and keep you covered."

"Thank you, my friend," Collin said, shaking Neo's hand.

Neo clasped Collin's hand in his. He had kind, grateful eyes. "You and your friend, God bless his soul, have helped many of our people go to America to find freedom. Your friend told me. You helped my brother go to America a few years ago, and he is doing well. My brother wrote to us, telling us of the kind American man who took them to land. He sends us American money and because of you and your friend, my family will be joining him one day soon. May God's speed be with you and keep you safe," Neo said. "Now let us go. We must go before they discover you are gone."

Chapter 29

Collin and Joey walked out onto the docks, trying to look as normal as possible. Joey walked tall, without the help of his brother, but Collin saw the strain on his face.

The dock held very few people, and these were poor workers. They kept to themselves, keeping their eyes purposefully away from what was going on. They didn't want to intrude or be witness to anyone's business.

The rain and fog were a blessing. As it was, the docks were already poorly lit with inadequate lighting. The walk to the boat wasn't far. Collin and Joey climbed aboard Adelio's boat and Neo nodded to them as he strolled past.

Joey collapsed on the boat while Collin, pulse racing, released the lines. They were far enough away from the warehouse now that they would not be noticed. A few boats came and went around them as the rain tended to bring good fishing. Adelio's boat eased away from the dock and quietly moved out into the open water.

They were ninety miles from home. Ninety miles to freedom. Joey badly needed a doctor. Could he make it home in time?

As soon as their boat was well within American waters, Collin got on the radio, begging for assistance from the Coast Guard.

He gripped the receiver and screamed through it, putting all his fear and relief into the call. "Mayday! Mayday! Mayday! This is Captain Collin Scott. Mayday! Mayday! Mayday! I am captaining the Adelio and need urgent help! Mayday! Mayday! Mayday! I require immediate assistance. Two people on board. One has been shot and is bleeding severely! Over!"

Once he'd made the mayday call on any frequency no other radio traffic would be permitted except to assist in the emergency. He would have the Coast Guard's full attention. They could launch helicopters and any other boats in the nearby vicinity to assist him. He would get the help he needed for Joey and everything would be fine. Joey would be okay.

Finally, after what felt like ages, the U.S. Coast Guard replied. Collin gave them his exact position and repeated the message that emergency assistance was needed as quickly as possible. The Coast Guard instructed Collin to continue on his current path and they would rendezvous with him soon.

"Joey! Everything is going to be okay," he called. "The Coast Guard is on their way!"

Joey was not looking good. In fact he was looking quite pale and seemed barely able to keep the shirt pressed against his wound.

Collin wanted to go to him, but he had to control the boat as well. He decided to try and distract him with stories.

"Joey! Hey, Joey! Do you remember the 'Bucket Story' Mom used to call it? Do you remember?" Collin was desperate to keep Joey's attention.

Joey mumbled something non-committal, but Collin kept it up, trying to stay calm for Joey. "Mom called us all into the house for dinner. You were only about five years old. I came rushing into the house and took my seat at the table. Mom looked at me, then she looked at Dad, and he just shrugged. They waited a few minutes for you to come in the door but you never did." He tried to laugh, tried to engage Joey, but everything he did sounded forced. "Mom asked me where you were. She was staring me down like a hawk, I tell you. She knew something wasn't right." Collin looked back over his shoulder at Joey and tried to laugh again. "I tried to keep from laughing and she told me to look at her. You know? The way she'd demand that and nobody on earth was going to look away after that? Anyway, she asked me again where you were and I told her you were in a tree. She looked at Dad, but he just sat back and folded his arms, waiting to hear what else I was going to say."

Joey made a grumbling noise that didn't resemble any kind of words. At least he was trying to be attentive as Collin told the story.

That was a good thing. Joey was staying as alert as he could.

"She told me to go tell you to come inside for dinner, but I said you couldn't because you were in the tree. Mom was getting upset by then and she asked me what I was talking about. So I told her you were hanging in the tree and couldn't come down. Dad started to laugh and I thought Mom was going to blow a fuse or something. Then she got up from the table and stomped through the house, heading out the back door."

Joey made a little chuckling sound when Collin looked back at him.

"Dad asked me what I had been up to and before I could answer him, Mom started screaming for him to come and help her get you out of the tree! Do you remember that?" Collin started really laughing now, unable to help himself. "Do you remember getting into the five gallon bucket and me hoisting you up with a rope tied to the handle?"

"At least you tied it to the tree with a good knot so I wouldn't fall," Joey managed. He laughed a little and grasped the shirt to his wound. "Stop! It really hurts when I laugh."

Chapter 30

When the Coast Guard arrived, approximately twenty miles from Key West, Collin and Joey were transferred to the Coast Guard's boat. Another boat towed Adelio's boat behind.

Collin held Joey's hand while two Emergency Medical Technicians administered first aid. At one point Collin looked up and recognized one of the U.S. Coast Guards on board, and the name Perez jumped to mind. He'd seen the man before during some of the Coast Guards' routine checks of fishing boats in the Florida Strait.

The technicians didn't move fast enough. Everything seemed to be progressing in slow motion. Collin was frantic. "He needs to get to a hospital! He needs a doctor!" he yelled. "Aren't you going to get a helicopter here?"

The two Coast Guards assessing Joey's wound exchanged a knowing glance but didn't speak. They continued to work on Joey but didn't look at Collin.

"Air support is on its way," one of the men said from behind him. It was an unsympathetic and cold reply and made Collin instantly suspicious. What did these guys know that they weren't telling him? Something was wrong, Collin thought to himself. Where was the damn helicopter?

Joey squeezed Collin's hand hard, sweating through the pain of the first aid as the two men applied pressure to his wound and prepped him for an I.V.

"You could have stopped this, Collin!" Joey sobbed. "It didn't have to be this way. We should have left. You promised to take me away from everything, just you and me. You promised! Do you even remember that?" He cried out, squeezing his face tight in agony, then went on, his words spitting out. "You said when the day came you would tell me it was time. Well, that day never came, did it? It's all your fault, Collin. I hate you," Joey managed. A line of blood started leaking out of his mouth. "Do you hear me? All of this is your fault!"

"What could I have done?" Tears flowed down Collin's face and he caught his breath in a hitch, trying to get his words out. "The yacht wasn't ready, Joey. What could I have done? Tell me what I could have done!" Collin pleaded, but he knew Joey couldn't possibly have an answer. No one could have done anything differently to change what had happened.

Joey blinked hard, struggling to look Collin directly in his eyes. "You could have stopped me from getting the mail," he growled, spitting out blood as his words came slower. He took short, quick breaths, and grasped weakly onto Collin's arm.

"What mail? What day are you talking about?" Collin asked softly. He was confused. What did Joey getting the mail have to do with anything? Maybe it was the loss of blood, the shock, the trauma that was getting to Joey.

"Today. The anniversary of Mom's and Dad's death. You should have stopped me from getting the mail today," Joey said slowly. His words began to fade. "But no. It's my fault. I shouldn't have yelled at you. I shouldn't have left you. I should have been more patient. I'm sorry, Collin. It's all my fault. I'm so sorry. Please forgive me."

"It's okay, Joey. It's okay," Collin said, not knowing what else to say. The E.M.T.s had stopped working and had moved away a bit, giving the brothers room. From the expressions on their faces, Collin surmised they'd done all they could do. Panic, grief and guilt roared through him.

He remembered the necklace Adelio had given him just before he'd died, the one his friend had said was a gift from his father. He slipped it off his neck and placed it on Joey, then held Joey's hand tighter. When the technicians didn't stop him, Collin slid his arm behind his brother's neck, cradling him, rocking back and forth. Joey took a sudden deep breath then his eyes rolled slightly back.

"No! Joey? Joey?" But Joey had died in his arms. Collin held his little brother's body against his own, sobbing helplessly. "Don't you do this to me, Joey! Don't you dare do this to me! Don't you leave me! Oh God! Why? Why? Joey! Joey!" he screamed.

As the boat neared land and police cars drove up with their sirens blaring, Collin still couldn't stop weeping. When the technicians came to take Joey's body, he didn't want to let go.

All at once, Collin was absolutely alone. He was suddenly aware that he would always be completely and utterly alone.

This couldn't be real. It had to be a nightmare. Had to be. Except he couldn't manage to wake up. He needed to wake up. Now. Please, Joey. Please!

He watched the technicians strap Joey to the stretcher. He felt weak, as if there was nothing left of him but guilt and misery. Then he felt a comforting hand on his shoulder, and looked through swollen eyes to see Perez standing there.

"He is with God now, my friend," Perez said in a soft voice. He frowned, examining Joey more closely. Before they could wheel him away, Perez touched the cross on Joey's chest. "Where did he get that necklace?" he asked.

A fresh wave of pain hit Collin and washed over him. "My friend gave it to me," Collin said, swallowing more tears.

"What is your friend's name?" Perez asked urgently, his voice a hoarse whisper.

"Adelio," Collin said slowly, remembering the last time he had seen his friend.

Tears immediately rose in Perez's eyes and started to trickle down his face. He swallowed hard, then reached for the cross around Joey's neck and gently turned it over. Under the bright lights, the name "Perez" was clearly visible, inscribed on the back of the cross.

"Perez. It is my family name." He stared at Collin. "Adelio is my son. My name is Gavin. Gavin Perez. Where is my son? Have you seen him? Please. You must tell me."

Collin blinked, stunned by the news. Would the pain never stop? His chin quivered madly and he turned away, unable to see any more anguish. He took a deep breath. "Adelio is dead."

Perez' entire body seemed to collapse in that moment. He dropped his chin to his chest, covered his face with his hands, and cried.

Chapter 31

He cried for the loss of his son. He cried for all the years he had not been able to contact his son so that he could tell him he had tried to get him to America legally. After he discovered his wife had died, Gavin had lost track of where Adelio had gone.

He cried for all the years he had lost and the knowledge that he would never again see his son. In his tortured memory he saw a brief image of young Adelio's smile when he'd first been given the family cross, then it was gone.

He cried for Collin and for Joey.

For the past five years Collin had met with Adelio so that they could transport Cubans to the freedom of which Gavin had always spoken.

For the past fifteen years, Adelio had thought his father had died trying to "sail to freedom".

All this time, Collin had been oblivious to the fact that Perez was Adelio's father. Things could have been so different. If Collin had known, he could have reunited Adelio and his father many years before.

Turned out, Collin could have helped Adelio's dream of freedom come true.

Now the only thing left of Adelio was his boat.

Perez stayed and listened to Collin's story as he told it to the police over several grueling hours of interrogation. Collin told the police everything: names, places, and dates. Collin knew he could be headed to prison, but he really didn't care anymore.

Through Collin's confession, Perez learned of the friendship and business arrangement which had existed between Collin and Adelio. Perez accompanied the police officer when he drove Collin home on what seemed like a never ending drive.

In the back seat of the cruiser, Gavin told Collin of his illegal exit from Cuba. He explained to Collin that he had specifically wanted Adelio to assist him in making the raft so he would know what to do in case Gavin did not survive the voyage and Adelio decided one day to attempt it. Collin told Gavin he knew the story up to the day when Perez had left Adelio and his mother in Cuba. It made Gavin happy to know that Adelio had remembered so well and shared the story. So he hadn't been forgotten after all.

Gavin had embarked on a six day journey across the Florida Strait, riding a tiny and shabby homemade raft. He had run out of water, food, strength and hope. When the Coast Guard finally found him, his body had been almost destroyed through sunburn and dehydration. He told them tales of waves as tall as buildings and described the sharks that had attacked his raft on his last night on the water. He would never forget the sound of their fins cutting through the calm sea.

Gavin was allowed to slip into society with little hassle as a sort of reward for having endured such a perilous journey. After securing a good job and gaining citizenship, which took many years, Perez went ahead with the process of legally bringing his wife and son to America. The paperwork was filed but no response was ever received. After years of trying to discover something, Gavin finally learned that his wife had died and the whereabouts of his son were unknown.

But Gavin never lost hope. He wanted to serve the great country that had taken him in and given him freedom.

He felt privileged to be able to work for the Coast Guard as a doctor. He wanted to work in the Florida Strait so that he could help other Cubans, and so he could watch for his son, if ever he dared to make the journey.

Gavin was now an American citizen. But he still did not dare travel to Cuba. Before he had left his country, Gavin had heard a well-known story about a man who had once gained U.S. citizenship after illegally leaving Cuba. The man had returned to his birth country many years later with plans to take his family back to America. As soon as the man landed on Cuban soil the authorities arrested him and sentenced him to twenty-five years in prison. Although the man was legally an American citizen, he had technically broken Cuban law and was punished with a long prison sentence to deter anyone else from leaving Cuba. Being an American citizen did not keep him from going to prison, and the United States could not come to his aid.

As of this evening, Gavin questioned everything. He had made the journey to America for his family but had never been able to bring them over. To discover that Collin had been Adelio's friend was amazing. Then he'd learned his son had only been about forty-five miles away from Key West, and he had been there two or three days a week. Gavin had lived with hope in his heart for all these years, only to discover that Adelio had been murdered on this night.

"Your fishing boat was found drifting without a crew and we feared the worse," Gavin told Collin. "It was towed to the ship impound yard for further investigation. However, because of the recent circumstances, my supervisor made a call and pulled a few strings. While you were being interviewed by the police, it was towed to the dock at your residence."

Gavin scribbled his phone number on a piece of paper and

handed it to Collin. "If I can ever be of any further assistance, please don't hesitate to contact me. Here is my phone number. When you are ready, I would very much like to sit down with you and talk more about Adelio." He put his hand on Collin's arm and squeezed. "And I would like to add that what you and my son did, well, I consider that to be both courageous and heroic. I am very proud of you both."

Collin hardly heard him.

The police car slowly turned into the driveway and Collin was finally home. It felt as if he'd been away for years. A dark, empty house waited for him.

Everyone he loved and cared about was gone, and all because of him. Mom, Dad, Joey, and Adelio were all dead. How could he go on living? What was he going to do now? He couldn't think. He didn't want to think.

Gavin shook Collin's hand, patted him on the shoulder, then stood watching as Collin turned and faced his dark house. Collin stared at the lifeless house, unable to move his legs. He didn't want to go in. Ever.

But as much as he didn't want it to, life went on. He had to move forward. Collin shoved his hands deep into his pockets and reluctantly wandered to the front door. The very door that Joey had slammed just this afternoon, frustrated at Collin's selfishness.

His mind drifted back to an evening when he and his mother had been sitting on the back patio, reading. On that particular evening one of her favorite songs was playing through the patio speakers. It was a calming, mellow tune. The kind Betty preferred when she was reading.

"I don't know what I would ever do without you, Mom," Collin had said.

"Life is precious, Collin, but you have to understand that life inevitably comes to an end," Betty replied. She closed her book and removed her reading glasses, then looked Collin directly in the eye. "One day your father and I will be gone. But you'll always have Joey," she had said, then smiled at Collin with her loving eyes. She touched his cheek.

"But you don't need to worry. You'll never be alone, Collin. By the time your father and I decide to leave this earth, you and Joey will both be long married and have several children." Betty giggled. "Hint, hint," she said. "I want some grandkids before I'm too old to spoil them."

Collin distinctly remembered walking away after their conversation was over and heading back inside. Just before he'd stepped into the house he paused to look over his shoulder. Collin smiled, content for a few moments to watch her read her book. A different song began to play softly through the speakers, and Collin sighed. He and Joey had wonderful parents.

He said nothing, only watched his mother for a moment, praying that he would never lose either her or his father. "I love you Mom," Collin had whispered under his breath. He didn't have to say it out loud. She knew he loved her.

But now, sitting alone at the kitchen table of his parents' house, Collin knew for the first time in his life, that his mother was wrong. She had said he would never be alone, but he was. Joey was gone. And Collin would give anything … anything to have him back. He would give anything to be able to tell his parents and Joey that he loved them.

What would his mother say to him now if she were here? Collin shook his head. He didn't want to think about her or his dad. He didn't want to think about Joey. He didn't want to think about anything ever again.

It wasn't fair. Life wasn't fair. What was the point of Collin's life? Of his going on without them? He wanted to be with his family and his friend. He wanted to die. Death would be easier than reliving the deaths of those he cared about every single day for the rest of his pointless, expendable life. And the burden of all that guilt was just too much.

The only friend Collin had left was alcohol. But Collin was too tired to even take a drink. He stumbled onto his boat and collapsed onto his bed. He grabbed a pillow and hugged it fiercely to his chest, curling around it as if to protect it. He buried his face into the soft white cotton and prayed this bad dream would just go away. Maybe, by the grace of God, he would never wake up. If he could simply lie there in bed and die in his sleep, that would be perfect.

He didn't think his eyes would ever close, but they did. Sleep finally consumed Collin's numb body and mind.

Chapter 32

What's that damn noise?

Collin lay in bed, rocking gently on his fishing boat, his mouth tasting like the inside of an old sock. Keeping his eyes squeezed safely shut against the possibility of bright sunshine, he stretched out one arm as he recognized the irritating beep of the alarm clock. His hand waved and fumbled around, trying to locate the snooze button, knocking over beer cans as he searched. Half a dozen cans crashed onto the floor next to his bed, then rolled around noisily while he continued to hunt for the snooze button.

Just ten more minutes. That's all I need. Within moments, the sounds of the water had rocked him back into a deep, peaceful sleep.

"Are you going to get up today?" a chipper voice called from above.

"Leave me alone," Collin grumbled, curling an extra pillow tighter under his arms.

"The sun is shining, the birds are chirping, and you're still asleep at two in the afternoon!" the voice practically sang. Whoever his tormentor was, he moved around as loudly as he could, banging boxes and pots, stomping heavily on deck.

Collin rolled over onto his back, arm slung over his eyes. "What day is it?" he managed.

"What day is it? It's Mom's and Dad's anniversary."

Anniversary? What in the world? Who was that? Collin shook his head, confused as everything from the night before flooded into his mind.

This had to be a dream. And he wanted it to go on forever. Because the voice calling down to him sounded exactly like Joey's voice, and that wasn't possible. Was this some sort of sick joke?

Collin swung his legs over the side of his bed and managed to stand, though his legs felt wobbly and weak. He glanced in the mirror to make sure he wasn't actually dreaming and combed his fingers absently through his hair, staring at his reflection with disgust. He was a mess. Not bothering to fix either his hair or his clothes, he climbed out of the boat and stepped onto the path to the house. By now he was practically vibrating with curiosity. Ignoring his pounding head, he raced up to the house and stumbled through the door.

He stopped short, staring at the apparition before him. Joey. It couldn't be possible. But there he was. Joey stood in front of him, as alive as he had been the morning before. Joey was alive! Had all this been a bad dream? Or was the alcohol playing with his mind? Could this possibly be real? Collin squeezed his hands against his temples, trying to hold in the confusion.

"Where's the Tylenol? I have a headache."

Joey was flipping through a book Collin hadn't seen before. Or maybe he had - just the morning before. "It's on the shelf, where you left it yesterday," Joey said sarcastically. He definitely had inherited his unique brand of sarcasm from their parents. "Are you going to work on the yacht today? It's going to be a great day. We could go get some more supplies if you need and I'd be glad to help."

"No, not today," Collin mumbled. He filled a glass with water, preparing to take his first dose of Tylenol for the day. "I have other things to do."

What was going on?

Suddenly Joey slammed his fist on the table, making Collin jump. "You know what, Collin? You always have other things to do! But here's the thing - I don't see you doing anything! Nothing! All you do is drink. You never used to drink. And I'm sick of it. I'm sick of your whole self-serving attitude, the whole poor me thing you're doing! They were my parents too, you know!" Joey shouted.

Collin flinched and closed his eyes. God, his head ached.

Joey kept on lecturing. "You don't see me moping around, feeling sorry for myself. Grow up, man. You're twenty-five years old, for Christ's sake! I'm only nineteen and I know you're acting like a baby."

Joey stood up, gaining momentum. He moved closer to Collin and jabbed one finger into his brother's chest. "You're supposed to be the adult, Collin. But in case you haven't noticed, I'm the one taking care of you. What would Mom and Dad say if they could see you now?"

"Look, you little bastard!" Collin shouted, reacting instinctively. "You don't have to take care of me! I'm doing just fine!" He turned toward the kitchen table, fighting a coughing fit.

"Oh, yeah," Joey replied, looking disgusted. "You sure do look like you're doing fine. You said you were going to fix up the yacht. You said you were going to take me away, that you and I were going to get out of this place and sail around the world. Forget everything that happened and be happy, out on the water, just you and me. That's what you said."

Joey's hands were squeezed into fists, his knuckles white with rage. "Were you lying to me? Come on, you idiot. It's been a year. An entire year. I've been waiting a year! Is that day ever going to come? Answer me, you fucking drunk!"

Collin froze, taking in everything Joey had just said. Almost everything had been true - except for the part about his being drunk. Collin hadn't had any alcohol in the last two days. Collin met his brother's gaze, then replied as calmly and as straight forward as he possibly could, given his current confused state of mind.

"When it's time, I'll tell you. Then we'll leave, no looking back. We'll just go, leave everything behind. I'll tell you when it's time."

Joey practically vibrated with fury. "Sounds like a bunch of bullshit to me!" he shouted. He got up and strode towards the front door, then looked back at Collin. "I'm going to get the damn mail. Do me a favor, would you, brother?" he said mockingly. "Try to pull yourself together. And do me another one. Take a shower. You smell like a fucking brewery!"

Then it all clicked into place. Déjà vu. Collin had heard of it, but never actually experienced it. His mother had told him that déjà vu was an experience in which a person was positive they had already experienced an event that was happening again at that moment. This seemed rather extreme, though. He had been under the impression that they could go for no more than a few seconds, though. But that's what it had to be. There was no other explanation.

Well, this time he could do something about it. Dream or not, this time Collin wasn't going to take any chances. The yacht was ready and fully equipped. It's time, thought Collin. It's time.

"Joey, wait. Just wait!"

Collin shouted at Joey, catching him just as he was walking out the front door. "I'm sorry, Joey. Listen to me. The yacht - it's ready. It's time. Do you hear me? It's time to go. We can leave right now if you're ready."

Joey stopped dead. After a moment he turned slowly, his hand still on the doorknob. He looked Collin straight in the eye, frowning suspiciously, but hope lurked behind the suspicion. "It's ready? It's time? Are you sure?" He took a tentative step closer to his brother. "You're saying we can leave? You and me? We can leave now?"

Collin's heart threatened to break yet again, seeing the distrust and welling tears in his brother's eyes. He knew Joey hadn't been able to depend on him over the past year.

"Yes, Joey. It's for real. Yes to all of it. It's time," Collin told him, a big smile growing across his face. He blinked against the onslaught of his own tears but was too late. He felt them rolling down his cheeks. Joey closed the gap between the brothers and Collin grabbed him tightly, never wanting to let go.

In Collin's recent memory he clearly recalled two final hugs with Joey. The first had been at their parents' funeral. The second had been in the moment that Joey had breathed his final breath. That

190

was never going to happen again.

"I love you, Joey. I'm sorry about everything that's been going on this year. I'm going to take care of you, you'll see. It's time. Let's go."

Joey squirmed. "Hey! You're squishing me. I can't breathe," Joey mumbled into Collin's shirt. Collin's laugh started from deep within, bubbling up as he let Joey go. Joey was grinning, too.

"Oh my God," Joey said, suddenly excited. "This is awesome. I have to get some things together. Clothes, and - oh, we'll need some food. My books, my laptop, and you'll have to get some stuff, too. This is so awesome. I can't believe it! We're finally leaving!" Joey glanced around the kitchen, finally grabbing a pad of paper on which their mother had made so many lists in the past. He started writing things down, his pen flying over the paper. "Jeez, man. You could have given me a little notice. It'll take half the day to pack!"

"No, Joey. We don't need to take anything," Collin said. "We're leaving everything behind. If we need anything we'll get it at the next port. It'll be okay. You'll see. Let's get going."

Joey looked uncertain. Collin was aware he wasn't making a lot of sense, but he wanted to get out of there before anything could happen. Of course Joey was expecting to at least take some of his things. But Collin couldn't wait.

"Well, at least let me check the mail," said Joey.

"No!" Collin cried, startling Joey. "There is nothing coming in the mail today. No packages being delivered and nothing of any importance. I'll contact Mom and Dad's estate attorney, and he will take care of every little thing. A management company will oversee the house, so we won't have to worry about anything. Our stuff will be packed up and put in storage and the house can be rented out to vacationers. Everything will be okay. Trust me. No worries."

"Okay," Joey said, sounding reluctant. Suddenly he seemed to be having trouble leaving everything behind, even though that's what they'd talked about all along.

"It's okay, Joey. I promise. I know you're scared, but I promise I'll look after things. I'll change."

As Collin's hand urged Joey toward the backdoor, he glanced out the bay window. A classic blue car slowed in front of the house but continued to drive past, not stopping. Collin inhaled, held his breath, then slowly let it out.

"Let's go kiddo."

Chapter 33

Joey hadn't stepped foot on the yacht since the death of their parents, and what he saw amazed him. Collin appeared to have covered every single detail. Joey wandered around, exploring all the fishing rods and equipment, scuba gear, and even the two Sea-Doo watercrafts. By the stern hung an emergency life raft with life vests. Collin had always been thorough.

The living quarters hadn't been ignored, either. Joey stared in awe as he walked through the doorway. A large, secured TV hung on the wall and a DVD player sat in the cabinet, stocked with hundreds of movies. Another cabinet was stocked with several of their favorite board games and a deck of playing cards.

Joey wandered over to the lower shelves, across the room from the L-shaped couch, mesmerized by the assortment of books he saw displayed. They had obviously been put there with Joey top of mind, because they ranged from marine life, plants, tides, and charts, to various other topics that had peaked Joey's interest in the past. He'd spent countless hours researching all this at the library. Now Collin had brought the library to him.

On the far wall hung a large framed portrait of their family. It was

Joey's favorite. The bookshelf below the portrait was filled by family photo albums he recognized from the house. Framed copies of the same photos that had been hung in the house were scattered around the living area.

"When did you get all this? You barely left the house to go anywhere." He frowned. "I can't believe I never noticed you bringing in all of this stuff!" Joey blurted, still looking around in amazement. "God, Collin. This is a dream come true! How did you do it?"

Collin shrugged, obviously pleased with Joey's reaction, but staying modest. "You went to the library every day. I ordered most everything online. All the packages and deliveries that came, those ones you were bugging me about? Well, this was what I was doing. All the food is non-perishable, of course. Mom stocked the basic items and I added more to them, stocking up for a long trip of some sort. When it was time, of course. The books were whatever I could remember you talking about after coming back from the library. I did some research of my own on oceanography, figuring out what was studied in the various related topics." He grinned at Joey's expression and clamped a hand on his younger brother's shoulder, guiding the way. "Come on. Let me show you your room."

Joey was shocked. The idea that Collin had done all of this by himself, without Joey's knowing anything about it, was absolutely unbelievable. And Joey had thought Collin had been doing nothing all this time but drinking himself into a stupor. When had he had the time to do all of this?

Joey's room was far more than he could ever have imagined. Collin had made sure it contained all the special, personal things and more. Mom had decorated the entire yacht, but Collin had stocked this room, customizing it for Joey. On the desk lay an iPod, a laptop, and a printer filled with paper. The desk drawer held rulers, gauges, pens, pencils, graph paper, notebooks and more. On the shelves lay oceanographer equipment: a Fathometer, a Salinometer, various measuring tools, thermometers, drift bottles, a few test kits, a microscope, GPS, and a compass. It was amazing. There was no other word for it.

Joey opened his closet and discovered all new clothes. More than he had in his own closet in the house. They still had the tags dangling from them. Joey had his own bathroom, well stocked with toiletries, towels, wash rags, a robe and slippers. Collin had thought of everything.

On the nightstand sat a small box with a card, next to a framed photo of their parents. Joey sat on the side of the bed and picked up the card. Before he opened it he took a deep breath. It had been an interesting year, and he had needed his brother very badly, but he'd been nowhere in sight. Now everything was changing, and he was going to get all he'd ever wanted and more. He opened the card and silently read it to himself.

Joey,

So you will always know where you're at, what time it is, and what day it is. You'll never be lost, and you'll never be alone.

Love, Collin

Joey swallowed hard. Tears filled his eyes so that everything blurred, as if he were looking through a kaleidoscope. He blinked, sending wetness streaming down his cheeks, but didn't bother wiping it away. Because for the first time in a very long time, they were tears of happiness.

Slowly, carefully, he opened the small box and stared at the treasure inside. After a moment he pulled out a Maxi Marine Divers' Watch and set it gently on his palm. He blinked tearfully up at Collin, shaking his head.

"This must have cost a fortune. Where did you get it? When did you get it? I don't know what to say. Thank you so, so much," Joey said. He grabbed Collin and hugged him. The brothers' tears soaked into each other's shirts, and neither one of them minded.

"Whoa. Now it's me that can't breathe."

Joey loosened his grip and smiled.

"Like I said, you can buy most anything on the internet," Collin answered softly, still holding onto Joey. "And Joey, you're worth every penny and more." He cleared his throat. "We have a satellite so you can continue your research and take online college classes. That way you can earn your Oceanographer's degree while we travel the world. You'll probably be at the top of your class, with all the specimens and testing you'll be able to document." Collin wiped his eyes with the back of his hand. "Let's go, shall we? We'll stop at the next port and stock up on some fresh food. And I know how much you love sugar and junk foods."

"Yeah. It's time to go," Joey said softly. He wiped his tears on his sleeve and began to smile, releasing his hold on Collin. He wasn't scared anymore. In a blink, Collin had returned to being the big brother he had been before. They would be close again. As close as any brothers could be.

As they pulled away from the dock, watching their home slowly fade into the distance, Collin asked himself for the thousandth time what was going on. Incredible as it seemed, could it all have been some kind of warning? Maybe from their parents, or maybe sent by God?

He watched the receding shoreline, still thinking. It had all seemed so real. Suddenly a thought struck him, jerking him into instant alertness. If Collin had changed the outcome and saved Joey from death ... could he also save Adelio?

"Joey!" he called abruptly. "Take the wheel! I have to make an urgent call to the Coast Guard." He turned, reaching for his cell phone, then took a few steps away.

"This is going to be awesome!" Joey said aloud, enjoying his new role. He was so excited he was barely listening to Collin's phone conversation.

"Yes! Yes!" Collin nearly yelled into the phone. "I need to speak to the Coast Guard! A supervisor, actually. Perez. I need Perez."

Joey glanced over, curious. Perez? What was Collin so excited about? He shrugged. Whatever. Collin would do what he needed to do. All that mattered was that they were leaving, actually doing this. Finally.

"Perez! Yes! I said Perez! He's a doctor for the Coast Guard on evening patrols in the Florida Strait."

"Who is Perez?" Joey asked. But Collin had turned away and was pacing the deck, throwing his hand up in the air as if he were getting frustrated with the person on the other end of the phone.

Then a big grin spread across his face. "Yes! Yes! That's him! Yes, Perez! I have a very important message for him. His patrol boat needs to rendezvous with a Cuban captain of the fishing boat 'Adelio' at five o'clock today," Collin said. He was speaking fast, which Joey knew meant he was getting impatient.

"This is Captain Collin Scott! He will know who I am. Oh! And one more thing!"

Joey was very curious now. The Coast Guard probably thought Collin had a screw loose or something. If Joey didn't understand what Collin was talking about, how could they?

Whatever it was, Collin was emphatic. "Tell Perez to make sure to inspect the necklace that the captain of the Adelio is wearing! Yes! I said the necklace! It is a cross, or a crucifix. It is imperative that he see it. This is vital." Collin threw his hand up in the air again, getting more upset by the second.

Joey frowned at him. "Calm down, Collin. Nobody can understand you when you talk like that. If it's that important, slow down!"

Collin frowned, then took a deep breath. "All right. Do you have that? Read it back to me, please." There was a pause while he listened, then nodded. "Yes. That's exactly right. Please make sure that he gets this message today. Right now, as a matter of fact. This is urgent. It's a life or death situation. Yes! You heard me correctly. I did say life or death!"

Collin's eye bugged with frustration. "I am sorry," he growled. "I didn't know it had to be a life or death situation in order to get an urgent message through to someone. Okay, fine. Just please make sure he gets the message. Thank you. Yes! Yes, that's right. Captain Collin Scott. Thanks again. Goodbye!"

Collin hung up, dropped the phone into his pocket, then turned to face a very curious Joey.

"What was that all about?"

"Checking the mail," Collin replied, grinning.

"Huh? What do you mean?"

"Joey, have I ever told you that checking the mail could change your life?" Collin raised an inquisitive eyebrow.

Joey frowned. "Are you sure you haven't had anything to drink?"

Collin laughed and set his hand on the top of Joey's head, tousling his hair. "I'm positive. It's a funny story, actually. I'll tell you all about it one day."

Collin pulled out a CD that had belonged to their parents and placed it in the CD player. The melody and the perfect words floated out through the speakers and for a moment he closed his eyes, thinking of Betty and George.

Collin smiled, watching Joey get familiar with the instruments and some of his new equipment. Today was a new beginning. A new future. Today they left everything behind. Today it was time. Today Collin knew what day it was.

Collin's eyes grew wide in thought, then said, "I need to make one more urgent call." Collin reached into his pocket, pulled out his phone, then looked at it. He hesitated for a moment, then slowly pushed the numbers on the keypad.

"Hello. Morgan? It's Collin."

The End

About the author - K.C. Hilton

Author of 'The Magic of Finkleton'

K.C. Hilton was born and raised in Aurora, Illinois. She spent her childhood playing street games with the neighborhood kids. When she wasn't outside, she spent much of her time reading and getting lost in adventurous worlds and whirlwind courtships. At the age of seventeen, she moved to Kentucky and eventually began to raise a family of her own.

K.C. has always been entranced by stories of magical adventure, and though she had to live in the practical world, running a family business as well as two of her own; she discovered that writing was an entirely new, exciting adventure all on its own!

K.C. has a large family and their get-togethers are so much fun! She is a photographer and takes tons of photos! Her family also has a mini dachshund; her name is "Roxy" weighing in at a whopping ten pounds. Roxy is a huge part of their family and she's is spoiled rotten!

Made in the USA
San Bernardino, CA
14 December 2012